BLIND FURY

A bullet slapped the sand six inches in front of Jim Winchester's face. He rolled to his left and curled up in a ball behind a stand of sage. He pawed desperately at his burning eyes and tried to open them, but he couldn't.

Winchester squeezed his eyes tight shut and prayed for the moisture that would wash the sand out. If only he had his canteen . . . but he had left it with his horse.

The sun baked down on him, and the minutes that passed seemed like hours. He was blinded, as helpless as a rabbit. He only hoped that the man in the rocks didn't know.

Winchester lay still and waited. In the next few minutes he would either open his eyes or die . . .

THE BEST IN WESTERNS FROM ZEBRA

BLOOD BOUNTY

BY DAN RABURN

ZEBRA BOOKS
KENSINGTON PUBLISHING CORP.

ZEBRA BOOKS

are published by

Kensington Publishing Corp.
475 Park Avenue South
New York, NY 10016

First printing: April 1985

Printed in the United States of America

Chapter 1

Amanda Strawbridge was so preoccupied with studying her complexion in the big mirror that she didn't hear the riders come up in the yard, but she heard them when they banged in the front door downstairs.

She sighed. Another unpleasant evening indoors, no doubt, listening to the low murmur of voices from Robert's study as he conducted yet another meeting with his designers and various other authorities on the Missouri river trade.

He was building another steamboat, the third in two years. One, she understood, that would displace less water and have greater maneuverability, better for the upper reaches of the Missouri where grounding and snags were the greatest hazard.

Amanda heard footfalls and voices downstairs as she finished applying her makeup. She studied her fortyish face in the mirror and pushed back a strand of reddish-brown hair that still showed no trace of gray. She was still a young woman, and not an unhandsome one.

She knew, however, that she had only herself to blame for Robert's inattention. It had been she who suggested they use their young nephew's inheritance for their own benefit after his parents were killed. One thing had led to another after that. They had never told the boy of his money . . . the same money that had made Robert and Amanda Strawbridge wealthy in the steamboat trade on the Missouri. And after the war James Winchester had, conveniently for them, disappeared.

All that they had heard from their nephew since had been rumor. It was said that during the war he was assigned to a group which tracked down deserters and spies, and he must have found the work to his liking, for when the war was over he had turned bounty hunter, a loner who hunted down and killed men for blood money.

Amanda shrugged the thoughts away and walked over to the window that looked out over the Missouri some five miles upstream of Council Bluffs. It was too late to cry over spilled milk. It was only a simple twist of fate, she tried to tell herself, but she knew inside it had been brought about by her own manipulation. They lived in a fine house and had prospered beyond what they had ever dreamed of in the beginning. And the man whose inheritance was responsible for it was now a killer who roamed the west sleeping beside lonely fires, completely ignorant of his own wealth.

She looked thoughtfully down at the three saddled horses in the yard. She frowned suddenly. Robert's

6

bay was not among them. She knew he had left on the bay. Why had he not returned on the same horse?

She dismissed the thought as unimportant and started to turn away from the window.

There was a crash downstairs and she jumped, startled. *What on earth?*

She heard footfalls on the stairs and, moments later, boots in the hallway.

Robert had never brought his guests upstairs before. They always went directly to his study where he offered everyone a drink and a cigar before they got down to business.

"Robert?" she called out.

There was no answer. Only more boots in the hall.

Amanda ran to the door and locked it, then backed away. Her hand sought the bureau drawer where she kept her derringer, and only after she opened it and felt inside did she remember that she had left the gun downstairs the last time Robert had been away at night.

She looked around the room for something else she might use for a weapon, but there was nothing—not even a hatpin. She seldom wore hats.

The window. If it came to it she could jump, but it was two floors up and she would surely break some bones.

"Robert?" she called again.

The crystal doorknob turned slowly, then creaked as someone applied a shoulder to it.

"Robert, if this is your idea of a joke, stop it at once!" She could hear the hysteria edging into her own voice as she spoke, and her heart began to thud heavily in her breast.

The door splintered and crashed inward, the thin deadbolt that had held it flying to bounce off the opposite wall and clatter on the floor.

A tall, whiplash of a man staggered in through the opening he had made and regained his balance. He was dusty and grimy and wore a stringy beard that did not cover a terrible scar that ran from the corner of his eye all the way down his cheek, losing itself only in the matted hair under his jawbone.

Two more men, just as dirty, came through the door behind him. When they saw Amanda they grinned at one another, and one spat a stream of tobacco juice against the wall.

"Well now," the tall one said, "I always heerd that when you found treasure you found it all at once. An' this here is what I call a real find."

"Amen, Brother Moses," the tobacco chewer said, "amen."

Amanda's skin crawled as the one called Moses' eyes raked her from head to toe, his gaze lingering longest on the cleavage presented by her low-cut evening gown.

She backed up against the wall beside the open window and twisted her neck to look out and down. Her eyes sought the distant ground, but as she saw the tall man take another step toward her out of the corner of her eye, the fall began to look less and less menacing.

"Wha—what do you want from me?" she said.

Scarface chuckled. "Why, just a little o' this and a little o' that, ain't that right, boys?"

The tobacco-chewer giggled mirthlessly . . . and at that moment she tried.

8

She whirled, stooped, and lunged as if she were diving into a pool. Her upper body cleared the window sill and she had made it . . . .

Her head and shoulders began to drop through the air, and relief surged through her . . . then a rough hand caught her ankle and jerked.

She was snapped back inside like an empty flour sack and hurled bodily across the room, landed half on and half off the big, four-poster bed.

She was dressed only in the flimsy blue gown and it had ridden up on her thighs. She struggled to pull it down, and the three men just stood and stared, struck dumb for a moment by the creamy whiteness of her limbs.

Then the tobacco-chewer started for her, but the scarfaced man shoved him back. "Wait outside," he barked, "an' don't come back in unless you hear somebody comin'!"

"Aw, Moses, how come you allus get first lick?"

Moses glared at him, and the tobacco-chewer's gaze faltered and he turned away. "Come on, Pete."

They filed out the splintered door dejectedly, and Moses turned his attention back to Amanda. He sat down on the edge of the bed.

She shrank away from him.

"Well, now, little lady—" his hand streaked out and flipped the gown back up over her knees and then fastened itself to the calf of her leg like a leech— "It'd be mighty foolish of you tryin' to run off anymore, 'cause ol' Mose is goin' to make you a happy woman."

She made no attempt to pull away from him. "Please," she breathed, "just take what you want and go. There's money and some jewelry in the safe downstairs — behind the big picture in the front room."

"Well, that's right nice of you, ma'am. Matter of fact, that's what we came for, but it looks like we found even more than what we expected." His hand began to stroke her calf, and he attempted a grin, but the scar that stiffened the side of his face merely turned it into a grimace.

Amanda shuddered and knew there was no use in fighting it. It would only make matters worse. If she should get away from this one there were two more just outside . . . waiting.

"Take it, then," she said, strangely calm. "And I'll even make a bargain with you."

"What's that, my dear," he crooned, his hand climbing and stroking her inner thighs.

"I'll make it good . . . I'll make it nice for you. I won't resist if you'll promise to keep the other two away from me."

He beamed. The idea had appealed to him, just as she had thought it might. Her hopes rose. Robert would never have to know. She would cleanse herself afterward and go out of the house and claim it had been robbed in her absence.

Scarface stood up and began to unbuckle his pants. He dropped his gunbelt and knife on the floor. "You're a real smart lady, yes indeedy."

Amanda tried to raise up to remove her gown but found that her body was frozen in fright, paralyzed as she watched him undress and reveal his dirty, scarred body. He was already aroused; his maleness protruded long and hard and knobby from his body.

He climbed on top of her and reached for the top

of her gown, ripped the thin material all the way down the front in one jerk and cast it aside in the same movement.

His twisted mouth came down hard on hers and his hands grasped her breasts and squeezed until she cried out. He opened her then like a partially healed wound, stabbed upward and inward, and she screamed with the dry pain of it. Nausea boiled up inside her and she twisted her head and vomited on the pillow.

The rest of it was only a bad dream. Consciousness came and went. At times there was only the dull aching inside her, and then the welcome blackness would envelop her again.

She thought she saw little Jimmy Winchester playing in the yard, and then he stopped his play and looked at her in that silent way she had always loathed. He had been a quiet child after his parents were killed, and there had been times when she had thought he would drive her insane with his solemn staring.

The tobacco-chewer and his friend Pete had slipped back into the bedroom and stood watching the pair on the bed ceremoniously.

Suddenly, their entertainment was interrupted by a voice that came from the stairs. "Mother, are you there?"

Moses' body stiffened, and he hissed at them, "Who the hell is that?"

"Don't worry, boss. We'll take care of it." The tobacco-chewer flattened himself against the wall beside the door and waited.

"Shit," Moses said. He climbed off Amanda and

11

jerked on his pants hurriedly.

"Mother?" the call came again. It was a girl's voice, closer now, coming up the hall.

The young woman came hesitantly to the bedroom door, and tobacco-chewer's arm shot out and grabbed her. She gasped and screamed as he pulled her inside.

The girl's wide eyes took in Amanda's nude body spread-eagled on the bed and the scarfaced man buckling his pants. She started to scream again, but the tobacco-chewer cut it short with a hand over her mouth.

"Tie her up," Moses ordered. "We're takin' her with us."

Tobacco-chewer pointed to Amanda. "But what about—"

"Go ahead," Moses said impatiently, "but make it snappy . . . an' kill her when you're finished."

"Right," tobacco-chewer grinned.

The one called Pete quickly ripped up a sheet and bound the girl's hands and feet. Tobacco-chewer shoved her down into a sitting position beside the wall. "There, honey, you sit and watch. Could be you'll learn something you might need a little later on."

Moses left them and went downstairs. There was a big picture of wild horses in a meadow over the fireplace. He threw it aside and fired three forty-five slugs into the lock of the miniature safe.

The door came open on the second tug, and he raked the contents of the tiny compartment out and stuffed it in his pockets—cash, a couple of pieces of jewelry, and some important looking papers. Those he would peruse later.

12

He took a quick look outside, then went back upstairs. Tobacco-chewer was just finishing up. He had slit Amanda's throat and she was bleeding profusely onto the bed, her mouth opening and closing like a chicken choking on a potato peel. She made wet, gagging sounds as she struggled to draw breath and choked on her own blood.

The girl on the floor was pale and looked as if she would faint any second.

Moses jerked her to her feet. "Let's git," he told the other two.

The girl struggled to speak and finally succeeded. "Are you — just going to — leave her like that?"

"Why, no, child." He drew the worn .45 from its holster.

The girl fainted, went slack in his arm, and Moses drew careful aim and fired.

Amanda took the bullet in the forehead, jumped with the impact of it, then relaxed.

They left the house then and rode southwest away from the river. The muddy Missouri rolled ponderously on, undisturbed and uncaring.

Chapter 2

Jim Winchester brought the dapple-gray gelding down off the barren slope and turned him up a dry wash. They followed a trail that was now less than an hour old and getting warmer by the minute. The man's wound had reopened, and the loss of blood was steadily slowing him.

It was only a matter of time. Winchester was finding a splotch on the sand about every fifty yards. The killer would have to stop and rest soon, try to close the bullet wound, or he would eventually fall out of the saddle.

It was unbearably hot. The sun burned like a torch in the brassy Dakota sky. To the east lay the cool Missouri river country, and westward lay the Black Hills, from where they had come.

The man he followed had killed the marshal in Deadwood while robbing the hardware store, but the killer had taken some lead himself before he got out of town. The folks in Deadwood were not pilgrims;

another shopkeeper across the street had emptied a rifle at the man as he fled town.

Winchester had himself heard the shots. They had awakened him from a sound sleep at the hotel, but he had dismissed them as the antics of a drunken miner and gone back to sleep.

But someone had heard that James Winchester was in town, and they had sent for him.

Just inside the wash, Winchester drew the gray up for a breather and took a swallow from his canteen. He grimaced at the metallic taste of the water and swallowed it slowly. He would have to go carefully now. A cornered man was as dangerous as any wild animal, and this one was no tinhorn.

Winchester swung his lean, six-foot frame down from the saddle and stretched. There was a three-day stubble on his face and his hair was long and unkempt. There had been no time for a barber in Deadwood.

He knelt and examined the newest splotch of blood in the sand. He rubbed the sand between a thumb and forefinger, and the blood smeared wet and not too sticky.

Fresh . . . very fresh.

His flat, black eyes searched the wash ahead. The killer could be just around the bend up there, more than likely *would* be. But he would not be in sight when Winchester rounded that bend. The man was no fool. He knew he had to stop and rest, but at the place where he stopped you could be sure he would be lying in ambush for anyone following.

And he knew he was being followed, Winchester was sure. Numerous times he had stopped in the last three days, turned his horse, looked over his back-trail.

He knew.

The sparest of smiles flickered over Winchester's weatherworn face, and he took the gray's reins and led him out of the wash the way they had come. He had hunted too many men in the last five years to fall for anything so simple.

There was no hurry now. He only had to wait, and patience he had learned well. Most men were impatient to a fault, and it had been the death of many.

He tied the gray in the meager shade provided by a straggly pine, pulled his .44 Henry out of the saddle boot, and proceeded on foot along the lip of the wash. In the holster at his waist was a short-barreled Colt .45 with the cutaway trigger-guard that saved a split second in drawing and firing, and in his business, a split second often meant the difference between life and death.

Would this man know any more than the others? Invariably the question popped into Winchester's mind. There was always that nagging hope that he had been unable to shake in five years of searching. And after each killing the answer was always the same. They didn't know what he was talking about — they had never seen such a man. Some even claimed to have seen him, thinking he might spare their lives if they had, but Winchester had always seen the lie in their eyes . . . and he had killed them and collected their rewards.

Somehow Winchester believed that if he ever found anyone who knew the whereabouts of the scarfaced man, the nightmares that had plagued him relent-

17

lessly for five years would cease.

Last night it had happened again, and it was always an exact duplicate of the dreams that had preceded it, never any different. He was a boy again, standing on the wharf at Council Bluffs watching the departure of the sidewheeler *Golden Boy*, one of the first engineered and built by his father. His aunt Amanda Strawbridge stood by his side as he waved goodbye to his father and mother. The boat was still so close that he could see the pained expression on his mother's face as she waved to him.

And then the boat erupted like a volcano, turned into a fireball as explosives planted in the hull turned the *Golden Boy* into a million pieces of kindling. The faces of his parents had disappeared forever in a dull thud on the face of the Missouri. The explosion shook the ground, and pieces of shrapnel and wood rained down upon those standing on the dock.

In his dream Winchester still heard the ladies on the dock screaming, and then the dream faded to the face of the scarfaced man. He had his head thrown back and he was laughing, a bellowing laugh that went on and on. The livid scar that ran from the corner of his eye all the way down his neck caused him to be unable to hold his head straight. He held it rather twisted to one side as he laughed, and his vicious grin stretched more to one side of his face than the other.

And then Winchester awakened in a cold sweat, just as he always did. After having the same dream two or three nights a week for five years, he had thought it might eventually cease to terrify him, but it never had.

And the hope was there again. As he walked cautiously along the edge of the wash, he could not drive away the thought that maybe this man would know something. Maybe this murderer would know something of his counterpart, a man with a terrible scar down the left side of his head, the man he believed was responsible for the death of his parents.

High above, a vulture circled slowly, exemplifying the patience of Job. It was watching the two men below. They each had weapons in their hands, and this could spell food for the vulture. It often had before.

Winchester rounded the bend in the wash and stopped. He squatted on his heels and mopped the perspiration from his forehead with a dirty bandanna. His eyes searched the sand below but saw nothing.

Ahead the dry wash played out and there was an outcropping of lava rock. Behind the rocks was another stand of pines with a couple of big boulders among them.

Damn!

The skin across Winchester's forehead tightened as he slowly began backing away. He was wide open to a shot from those rocks. If the man hadn't seen him it was only because his attention was focused on the wash, as Winchester's own had been.

He backed off slowly, one easy step at a time, careful not to make any sudden movement that would draw attention. The longing in him was to turn and run, but he knew that it would be a deadly mistake.

Suddenly, a horse nickered a greeting from over in the rocks, and in the same instant Winchester tripped over something and fell.

A bullet slapped the air where his head had been, and the sharp report of a rifle followed.

Ten feet and he would be over the crest of the knoll and out of sight. Winchester allowed the momentum of his fall to cascade him into a roll. Another bullet showered him with sand, and then he was out of range.

He got up and sprinted on down the slope to the tree where he had left the gray. He had miraculously managed to hold onto his rifle. He shoved it in the boot and mounted up.

He turned the horse and skirted the base of the knoll, approached the back side of the rock outcropping and dismounted again. He bellied down in the sage and started crawling, Apache-style, toward the stand of pines.

The element of surprise was gone, and Winchester didn't like it . . . not at all. It lessened his chances for speaking to the man before he killed him.

Now it was down to simple, guerrilla warfare, and it was probably this that Winchester knew better than anything. No one was better at guerrilla fighting than the Apaches, and he had lived among them once down in Arizona.

He belly crawled almost ten yards through the bunch grass, then rolled six feet to his left behind a clump of sage.

There was no sound from the rocks.

Winchester mopped the sweat out of his eyes again. He was only thirty yards from the rocks. He covered another five yards, rolled, and waited.

Still nothing.

Surely the man had heard his horse and would have been watching his back. Was the man already unconscious from loss of blood, or had he merely overestimated him?

Winchester moved to crawl again—and a bullet slapped the sand six inches in front of his face.

Jesus shit!

He rolled to his left and curled up in a ball behind another stand of sage. He pawed desperately at his burning eyes and tried to open them, but he could not.

He squeezed them tight shut and prayed for the moisture that would wash the sand out. If only he had his canteen . . . but he had left it with his horse.

The sun baked down on him, and the minutes that passed seemed like hours. He was blinded, as helpless as a rabbit. He only prayed that the man in the rocks didn't know.

He lay still and waited. He thought he could have died a thousand deaths over the next five minutes, wondering if the killer was walking up on him. He gripped the Henry tightly and sweated, listened intently for any sound.

His eyes watered fiercely, and at last his vision began to return. He mopped the streams of gritty water from his face and tried to think. Had the thought earlier crossed his mind that he might have *overestimated* the man in the rocks?

A breeze stirred in the pines and Winchester felt the whisper of it on his cheek. He stared long at the rocks and trees but saw nothing. Obviously the killer was in no hurry, either, and he had something that Winchester did not. He had the shade.

21

Suddenly, he thought he saw a movement and looked again. A hat was beginning to protrude over the top of a boulder in the pines. It was still a moment, then the breeze stirred again and the hat wobbled slightly.

He smiled. Suspended on a stick or a rifle barrel, probably. The man was testing him, trying to find out how much of a tinhorn he was, testing his patience.

Winchester abruptly decided to mislead him. He drew a careful bead and fired.

The hat went flying, and he rolled to his left again as soon as he squeezed off the shot.

A bullet kicked up sand in the spot he had just vacated.

"Mister!" Winchester called out, just loud enough for his voice to carry, "I'm looking for a man. You tell me where I can find him and I'll ride out and leave you be."

There was a long stillness, and just when he thought there was going to be no reply, a worn voice called back. "I know who you are, Winchester — and you can go straight to hell. I don't know anything about any scarfaced man and if I did you still wouldn't leave without collecting my reward."

"How do you know about Scarface?"

The killer laughed humorlessly. "You don't know me, Winchester, but I remember you. You didn't know anyone was around listening, but I heard you make a friend of mine the same deal once. He told you where you could find the Scarface, and as soon as the words were out of his mouth, you shot him deader'n shit."

"He was lying through his teeth."

"You don't know that and neither do I. But you and I aren't going to have any secrets from one another, friend. It's just you an' me, boy. You're out to kill me and collect a bounty, and I'm out to stop you. So get on with it."

Winchester came up with legs churning, snapped off a shot at the boulder, fell and rolled.

Then, as he gathered his wind, he heard a noise and looked up to see the man coming at him—only twenty feet away and covering ground. His left arm was in a bloody bandage and his teeth were bared in a death grin. The pistol in his right hand spewed lead.

Winchester came to his knees and, just as he lifted the Henry, a bullet slapped his left arm and knocked him flat.

The death grin grew wider as the man threw down on him from ten feet and squeezed the trigger.

Winchester fired in the same instant, and the impact of the .44 lifted the man off his feet as his own bullet threw up dirt between Winchester's outstretched legs.

Still the man did not go down. He lifted the pistol for another shot.

Winchester fired again, and the heavy .44 slug smashed the death grin from the man's face. Bits of teeth flew like tiny bits of gravel, and blood and gray matter sprayed out behind the killer as the bullet took away the back of his head.

Winchester's left arm began to pain, and when he gripped the bicep with his right hand, blood oozed between his fingers. His head fell back on the sand, and he stared up at the vulture that still circled in the brassy sky. He struggled to hang on to consciousness as the shock wore off.

He passed out briefly, and the scarfaced man began to laugh again. He was standing on the banks of the Missouri, head thrown back and roaring his laughter out over the water.

Winchester snapped back to and shook his head to clear it. He forced himself to his feet and staggered back to his horse, took the canteen and swallowed a mouthful of the brackish water and felt a little better.

He tore the arm of the shirt and inspected the wound. The bullet had only passed through the meaty part of his upper arm, scarcely more than under the skin, but the flesh around the wound was already red and inflamed. For lack of anything else, he poured a little water through the hole, then bound the arm tightly with a piece of his shirt.

He went back to the dead man and looked down at him. He was an old man, old enough to be his father. Fifty-five, maybe sixty. The face, Winchester thought, except for its present disfigurement, might have been a kindly one.

But he had not been kind to the marshal in Deadwood, had he? Winchester shook his head, angry with himself. The man was a killer, nothing more.

He walked to the copse of pines and located the man's horse, ground-hobbled in the dry wash in back of them. He led the animal out and spoke soothingly to it.

It was a piebald gelding, stocky and short-legged, a mountain bred horse unsuited for this part of the country. For the vast expanse of plain and rolling hills of the Dakota territory a man needed a big horse like

Winchester's gray, long of wind and limb, and with a ground-eating stride. The piebald was dusty and trail worn; its ribs were beginning to show.

Winchester went through the saddle bags on the horse, then through the dead man's pockets. He found about fifty dollars that had probably been taken from the hardware store in Deadwood, but no identification.

He took the blanket roll from the piebald, spread it out and tied it around the corpse's upper body and shattered skull to keep the flies from blowing, then he loaded the body across the horse and secured it to the saddle.

The fifty dollars he would keep along with the five-hundred he had coming from the citizens of Deadwood. The body he would take back to those good people so they could see what their money had bought them — another dead man. An eye for an eye . . . that's what they said they wanted, and he wanted them to see the results.

Winchester mounted the gray and took up the reins of the piebald, and they went up the dry wash and headed west.

Behind them, the turkey vulture slowly settled to the ground. He landed on the spot where the killer had died, turned a baleful eye in the direction the men had gone, then pecked viciously at a piece of the dead man's brains that lay drying in the sand.

Chapter 3

Deadwood was a roughshod boomtown that had grown almost overnight into the nucleus of Black Hills mining since the discovery of gold there. It was the hub around which the miners revolved. New buildings were being erected almost weekly to house the influx of beer-swilling miners. The string of saloons and pleasure houses was interrupted occasionally by an assay office, and there were two hardware stores which dealt principally in mining equipment.

When Winchester rode in the third morning after killing the man in the dry wash, the streets were teeming with men and wagons. Shovels and picks clanged here and there and the men called to one another good naturedly.

Some distance away, the smell of fresh coffee brewing came to him on the morning air, and his stomach growled in anticipation.

It had rained the previous night, and the street he

approached was soupy with mud. It streamed from the wheels of the rolling wagons and spattered under the feet of the horses.

Winchester rode slowly down the middle of the street leading the piebald, and there was a perceptible lull in the confusion as heads turned to look.

Flies buzzed around the bloodstain that had soaked through the blanket the dead man was wrapped in, and the piebald kept swishing his tail at them.

Winchester now sported over a week's growth of beard, and his face was drawn and haggard. The flesh wound of his arm was healing nicely, but it had taken its toll on his strength. His black eyes were mere slits, and he was in bad need of a good meal and a soft bed.

He dismounted in front of the hardware store and had to catch on to the pommel of his saddle as his knees buckled just a little.

He cut the thongs that held the corpse on the horse, led the piebald alongside the hardware store, and shoved the body off against the wall. It landed with a sickening thud in the mud and fell over sideways in the same position it had been on the horse, clawlike hands reaching for the ankles.

He then led the two horses on down the street to the livery. He could feel the eyes on him everywhere. No one stared openly, but covertly out of the corners of their eyes. And the looks were not friendly; they were fearful and distrustful, some, he knew, even filled with hate.

It was as he had known it would be. They had wanted him at the time the crime had occurred, had been eager and willing to pay for his services. But

28

now that the job was completed they hated him for it . . . and themselves. It was he who had pulled the trigger, but sómewhere deep inside, they knew it was they who had caused the deed to be done, and they did not like that feeling.

Winchester left the hostler instructions to grain and rub down the horses, paid him in advance, then walked back to the hardware store.

A group of men had gathered around, their eyes downcast. They were talking among themselves but seemed to have having trouble looking at one another. Winchester recognized a couple as being on the committee which had hired him.

"There's your man," Winchester said, to no one in particular. "I'd like to have my money today. I'm going to be moving on."

A short, fat man who seemed to feel important spoke. "We'll call a council meeting and get the money together."

"Bring it to me at the hotel. I'm going to rest up a little."

The fat man pointed to the body. "Meantime," he said, "what do you think we're going to do with *that*?"

"That," Winchester said coldly, "is your problem."

He walked away toward the hotel and left them standing there. It was apparent that the fat man did not like the idea of handling that body — not even a little bit.

He stopped in front of the hotel and started to open the door, then he changed his mind suddenly and walked on down the street. He carried the Henry loosely in his left hand.

It had been a year since he had seen her, and a lot of things could happen in a year. She could have moved on, as he had done, or she might have found herself a man . . . a steady man, that is. But Winchester doubted it. Not her.

The little two room shack that he remembered on the south side of town hove into view and he grinned. It was exactly as he recalled, part soddy and part clapboard, and someone still lived there. The yard was swept clean and there were flowers growing in front. Smoke rose lazily from the chimney.

He rapped on the door, still grinning, and a whiskey voice yelled from within. "Who the hell is it?"

"Come an' see, darlin'."

"Darlin'! Why, you no good, penny-ante, gold-grubbin' drunk! You wouldn't know a darlin' from the end of a muck stick. You—"

The door flew open and she stood there, illuminated in shocking detail by the morning light, clothed in only a makeshift gown. Her breasts were still big and firm and the shock of unruly blond hair was the same. She was older than he was, maybe thirty-five, but the only difference he saw in her was a few wrinkles around her eyes that had not been there a year ago.

Her mouth fell open at the sight of him.

"Hello, Rose."

Her pale blue eyes blinked back tears and her chin quivered. Finally she found her voice. "Well, I'll be damned . . . Jim. You're the last person in the world I expected to see."

He grinned. "I can tell." He stepped into her arms, and she hugged him fiercely.

30

Her shoulders contracted and she stifled a sob against his shirt. "Jim Winchester, goddamn you, it's been so fucking long."

"Hey, hey!" He pushed her away gently. He had known she had liked him, as much as he had her, but this— "What's got into you? This is not the Rose I knew. Where's that tough ol' gal from last year—old devil-may-care Rosie?"

She laughed and pulled away from him, drying her eyes. "She's still here. It's just that I heard you were in town a week ago and I guess I kind of expected you to drop by, and when you didn't I just—" She shrugged and dropped it lamely.

"Don't tell me you're getting sentimental in your old age," he chided, and closed the door behind him.

"Maybe I am, I don't know. The toughness seems to kind of wear off after you've been out of the business for a while." She looked at him levelly. "You did hear that I wasn't ridin' the same circuit anymore, didn't you?"

He looked around the room. It had not occurred to him before, but everything *was* still the same . . . and it shouldn't be, not in Rose McEachen's business.

The floor was only hard-packed earth, and the walls papered in some aged pattern, cracking and falling off in places.

The brass bed in the corner was freshly made, and there was no evidence that she had had any visitors lately. No lingering smell of cigarette or cigar smoke.

On the stove a kettle of water steamed, and against the wall were a half-dozen wicker baskets of dirty laundry. Beside them was a tub and a scrub board.

The woman looked disappointed at his obvious

31

confusion. "I thought you might have heard," she said. "I'm not doing that for a living anymore, Jim. I'm—I'm taking in laundry."

"Laundry?" He was stunned.

She shrugged. "It's probably no more respectable than my old profession, but at least the local church-goers don't try to run me out of town."

He merely stood and looked, unsure of what to say.

She became angry then. "Well, don't look so god-damned shocked. You think I was goin' to be a whore all my life? Five more years and I would have been washed up, anyway. It's a man's world out there. What the hell is a girl supposed to do?"

He tried to regain his composure and managed a small smile. "Well, do you think you could make an exception for an old friend?"

She stared at him for a moment.

He shuffled his feet and looked at the floor. She did not answer, and he turned and headed blindly for the door. "Sorry, Rose. I—"

As his hand touched the doorknob she burst out laughing.

He turned around, and she took his arm and led him to the bed, turned and put her arms around his neck. "You don't have to act like you just ran into the parson or something. It's not like that. Nothing's changed between us, Jim. I'm just not a whore anymore, and I don't want you to think of me that way."

She undressed in silence, and he sat down numbly on the side of the bed and watched her. Her body was still young and supple. Her breasts sagged only slightly, and as she lay down on the bed and stretched out for his appraisal he felt the hot need for her rising in him. It had been a long time since he had last felt the need for a woman.

He undressed and lay down beside her and her eyes stared hungrily at his rising manhood. "And you know something else?" she said softly.

"What's that?"

"No charge this time."

She laughed again, and this time he laughed with her, remembering the first time they had met.

She reached for him and pressed her mouth to his urgently, sobbed again in her desperate need. "Love me," she said, "oh, hurry."

He did, and it was like nothing he had ever known from Rosie McEachen before. It was then that he believed all she had told him was true. It was as if it had been as long for her as it had for him, and it showed. She literally struggled against him, violently and in desperation, and when at last she was fulfilled she cried out her relief to the dilapidated room.

Afterward, they talked a little and then he slept. He was already dead tired, and the lovemaking had exhausted him.

It was late that evening before he awoke, and he sat up groggily and blinked his eyes, unsure of where he was.

Then he remembered.

Rose was at the stove, stirring something in a kettle that smelled so good it set his stomach to growling anew, and he remembered that he had not eaten since yesterday. It was the smell that had awakened him.

She was barefooted and wearing a fresh gingham dress that clung to her in all the right places. Her hair,

33

too, he noticed, was freshly washed and combed.

He leaned back on the heels of his hands and simply admired the wonderful curve of her buttocks for a moment. He suddenly felt like a fool for staying away so long. Despite her sordid past, which was certainly no worse than his own, she was still a fine looking woman.

She heard him stirring behind her and turned around. "Awake, are you?"

"Barely."

"It's a good thing, too. I was about to check your pulse to see if you had died. How long since you slept?"

"Only dozed a little the past two—three days."

She looked at him. "Why, for God's sake?"

He shrugged. "I don't sleep too well around dead folks." He told her briefly of bringing the marshal's killer back to town, sparing many of the details even though it wasn't necessary. There was no need trying to hide anything from Rose. She knew him, well enough. Why she thought as much of him as she did he had stopped trying to figure out a long time ago.

She merely shook her head and didn't speak for a moment, then she came and sat beside him on the bed. "You're still looking for that man, aren't you, Jim?"

He nodded. "I will be until I find him. You know that."

"And what then?" she asked quietly.

"Don't start that again, Rosie. Don't try to pick my mind apart. It's just something that I've got to do before I can ever do anything else."

"You're becoming something of a legend, you

34

know," she went on, "only not in the same vein as Hickock or Earp. You're not the idol of any little boy anywhere. The only thing your name arouses in men or boys is fear—fear of the violence and killing that rides with you. Every outlaw in the west is terrified of the name Winchester because any one of them could be your next victim. And the decent people fear you as well, because your gun seems to bear no loyalty to anyone. I—"

"Stop it, Rosie," Winchester snapped, suddenly angry. "Just stop it. We've been through all of this before, and you know it's not going to do any good."

She sighed. "I know. I'm sorry. You're right, I should have known better after all this time."

After a moment, he took her hand and kissed her gently. In another moment, she slipped out of the dress and dropped it on the floor, pushed him easily back on the bed and lowered her body over his.

They made love again, and soon afterward, his hunger became more insistent and he got up and dressed. She set two plates on the rickety table in the front room and ladled out the stew she had been cooking earlier.

They ate the stew and drank coffee in silence, and Winchester noticed that he was relaxing for the first time in weeks, the tension slipping out of him by degrees.

He sat back in his chair and regarded the woman across from him soberly as she sipped her coffee. "You doin' all right?" he asked. "I mean—you need any money or anything?"

"No. I'm okay, I guess."

Silence again. Winchester looked around the room.

35

It was getting dark. He had slept the whole day away. He got up and lit the lamp and a yellow glow filled the small room.

Rose's tousled blond hair shone in the lamplight as she ran her fingers through it. She got up and began to clear the dishes away. "Money," she said stiffly, "is not what I need."

Someone knocked at the door then, and Winchester went to open it.

A freckled boy in tattered breeches handed him an envelope. "James Winchester?" he piped.

"Yeah?"

"Some messages for you, sir."

"Thanks, kid."

The boy's expectant smile faded and he stuck out his tongue as Winchester turned his back and closed the door on him.

In the first envelope was the five-hundred dollars that was owed him, no message attached. The second was a letter, soiled from numerous handlings and with several postmarks. The first, he noticed, had been at Council Bluffs, Iowa almost four weeks ago.

He frowned and ripped it open.

Rose glanced at him, sniffed, then turned her back again and pretended to be disinterested.

The letter was short and plaintive. The major body of it scarcely even perturbed him. It was from Robert Strawbridge and informed him that his aunt Amanda had been raped and murdered.

Served the old biddy right.

He read on, and when he came to the last line his breath caught in his throat.

Believe scarfaced man to be involved. Need your

36

help.

He pocketed the money he held and tossed his uncle's letter in the stove.

"I've got to go, Rosie."

She whirled on him, her eyes wide. "Just like that — just like before?"

"No time to explain."

"You've *never* any time." Her voice began to climb. "But you had enough time a few minutes ago, didn't you? Maybe next time I won't have enough time for you."

"I'm sorry, Rosie. It's just the circumstances — the fall of the cards."

"I'm not playing cards here, goddamnit!"

"I never promised you anything, Rosie," he said evenly.

She took a step back and looked at him. "So that's it," she said at last, her voice strangely calm. "Slam-bam-thankee-ma'am. That's all it was to you all along, wasn't it?"

He went and put his arms around her, but she was stiff and unyielding against him.

"No, Rose, that's not it. I can't explain now. But I'll be back soon. I promise."

She merely stared at him, eyes wide with disbelief.

He turned away from her and went out the door, headed for the livery stable where he had left his horse.

Along the street he saw the boy who had brought him the letter. The kid was gouging up mud balls with his big toe and kicking them.

Winchester stopped and dug in his pocket, handed the boy a coin. "Here, kid, get outa the mud. Go buy yourself some licorice."

"Gee, thanks, mister."

He ran off and Winchester looked after him and shook his head. Goddamn kids nowadays expected pay for everything.

It was getting late and the hostler was nowhere to be found at the livery, so he saddled his own horse and rode out of town at a gallop, headed into the badlands the way he had come.

Since he had already slept he would ride most of the night, stop just before dawn and maybe sleep a couple of hours before going on.

On the south side of Deadwood, Rose McEachen walked out into her yard and listened to the hoofbeats fade into the night. In her hand she clutched a half-burned sheet of crumpled paper.

Chapter 4

If her feet had not been tied underneath the horse, Julia Strawbridge did not think she would have been able to stay in the saddle. She had slept little in three days, and had eaten almost not at all.

Her hands had long since become numb and bloodless where they were tied too tightly behind her, but she dared not say anything. She had already stopped trying to talk to her captors. When she had tried to be civil with them, they had taken it as an invitation for their roaming hands, and when she had shown hostility toward them, she had been cursed, spat upon, and beaten.

She had spent so many hours blindfolded that she had become disoriented and no longer knew how many days it had been since her mother was killed and she had been abducted. She thought five, but it could have been as many as seven or eight.

Julia tried to move in the saddle and grimaced with pain. There wasn't a muscle in her body which didn't ache, or a bone which wasn't bruised and sore. Her backside was a pure agony. She had ridden before, but never this long at once.

The leader, Moses Gann, rode ahead of her, and the other two behind. Julia did not know what Moses had over the others, but so far he had managed to keep them at arm's length of her. He could not keep them away completely, and he didn't try, but at least she had not been raped . . . yet.

The tobacco-chewer, or Hiram she had heard him called, she had come to hate passionately. He was the worst of the three. She believed all he ever thought of now was her body, and all he had ever said to her had been something crude and suggestive.

His eyes were upon her now. She could feel them burning into her flesh, and she felt her skin start to crawl again.

She had not been told where they were going, but somehow she gathered, by the way the men acted, that they were almost there. They rode toward the west, she knew, because the sun was setting there behind the rolling hills. Somewhere behind them lay the Missouri, then. Those were the only two coordinates she had. Other than that she was totally lost.

Julia heard hoofbeats drawing closer as one of the mounts behind her started moving up. Her heart sank.

Hiram again.

He pulled his horse up alongside her and grinned, spat a stream of tobacco juice to the off side. "How you doin', sweetie? Butt sore?"

She nodded, but kept her eyes straight ahead.

He giggled and reached toward her suddenly. His

hand fastened on her breast, and he pinched the nipple, hard.

She almost fainted with the pain of it, but she did not cry out. Her breasts were terribly sore from the ill treatment they had received over the past week, the nipples so tender she could scarcely bear to touch them herself.

Hiram rubbed the spot he had pinched gently as if to soothe the injury, and giggled again. "That's it," he said, "you just keep on bein' a good girl. One of these days me an' you are goin' to have some real hot times together. Ol' Moses up there," he confided, "is gonna have things to do. He's not always going to be around to look after his little girl."

Julia cursed him silently, her lips moving.

"What'd you say, sweetie?"

She shook her head, praying he wouldn't guess.

Hiram reached out a hand to stroke her breast again.

Julia swallowed hard and tried to speak. "Pl—please," she managed at last.

He hesitated. "Please what, sweetie?"

"Don't pinch me again . . . please. I can't take it, anymore."

Hiram started to giggle again, uncontrollably. His hand fastened itself to her breast, and he pinched, harder this time.

Julia screamed. Pain shot through her like a hot-bladed knife, and she tried to wrench away from him but could not. She felt faint and sick, and she fell over her horse's neck and retched.

Ahead of them, Moses Gann stopped his horse and twisted around in the saddle. His eyes were furious, and a bad nerve pulled at the scar on his face. "Goddamnit, Hiram, leave that girl alone!"

"Aw, Mose, I was just funnin'."

"I know what you was doin'. You've been tormenting that girl for a week, and I'm tired of listenin' to your silly-ass giggling and her squeals. Now leave her alone awhile."

"Sure, Mose, sure. Take it easy. I was just funnin'."

Moses turned around and started moving again. They were getting farther away from the river and deeper into the hill country. The sky overhead was darkening rapidly as the sun finally sank out of sight.

Julia sighed with relief as darkness gathered around them. Soon they would sleep, and she would be left alone for a few hours, but when the hated light of day came again, she would be another twelve hours in Hiram's hell.

But as the minutes passed she began to grow alarmed. Full darkness had fallen and still they had not stopped for the night.

They rode on as the moon rose, and Julia fell over her horse's neck in weariness. Her brain became numb with the steady clop, clop of the horses' hooves and the relentless pain in her body.

Suddenly, as if awakening from a dream, she became aware that they were no longer moving. Her horse had stopped walking. Ahead of her, Moses was dismounting.

The ties that held her feet were cut and she was jerked bodily out of the saddle. After the long hours aboard the horse her legs were weak and refused to support her. She fell flat on her face and simply lay there; the hard, still ground felt wonderful underneath.

Hiram and the one called Pete grabbed her arms, one on each side, and jerked her up.

Dimly, ahead of them in the waning moonlight, Julia thought she saw a shelter. They had ridden into a draw between two knolls, and in one of the cutbanks there was a dugout.

The place was cither a dry streambed or had been created long ago by a flash flood. Only water could have fashioned the sheer banks on each side. The knolls between which the draw lay were heavily wooded.

A large boulder stood in front of the doorway to the dugout, and opposite it was a deadfall that had tumbled from the bank above, obscuring the door from view if approached from the other direction. If Julia had not known something was there, she could easily have ridden by oblivious to its presence.

And so, probably, would anyone else.

She stifled a sob. If anyone were following them, they would never find her here.

Were they looking for her, even now? She doubted it. It had been a week or more, and two days ago it had rained. She was sure that any tracks they had left were gone now, and if there was nothing left for them to follow, what could they do?

The men dragged her inside the dugout and threw her in the nearest corner. It was pitch black inside and smelled strongly of woodsmoke and kerosene.

A match was lit and touched to the wick of a lamp. The dugout, she saw, was all dirt and shored up with timbers. There was a stone fireplace against the back wall; the smoke from it probably rose to dissipate in the timber on the knoll above them.

Around the fireplace were a couple of wooden benches, and there was a single table on which the lamp set. In the corner was a pile of ratty buffalo robes.

Moses Gann came toward her with a short length of rope and bound her feet again, but not as tightly this time. He also loosened her hands a little, and she worked them to return the circulation.

"What," she asked Scarface under her breath, "do you intend to do with me?"

"Never you mind," he said. "But I will give you a piece of advice. Keep your mouth shut and don't try anything funny and I'll see that nothing happens to you. Try to get away and I'll turn you over to Hiram. You got that?"

She nodded numbly.

"Your father," he went on, "is a mighty rich man, and I aim for him to turn his pockets out and shake 'em."

"And what if he won't?"

Scarface shrugged, cast a glance at Hiram, looked back at her and grinned.

A shiver went through her, and she drew her knees up and locked her arms around them.

There were provisions already in the dugout, and the men started a fire and set about cooking some bacon and beans.

Moses sat down at the table and pulled some crumpled papers out of his pocket and started looking through them. Julia did not recognize the documents, but she suspected they had been stolen from the house when they had killed her mother.

44

Jim Winchester.

She was startled as the name came to her out of nowhere. He was a cousin that she had not seen since she was a child. He had lived with them up until he had gone away, and she remembered that she had hated him when she was a little girl. He had been older than she, a strange and quiet boy, and she had been afraid of him.

She had overheard her mother and father talking about him a few times, and she had heard rumors from other sources as well, when they had not known she was listening.

He was a bounty hunter, they said, a cold-blooded killer that not even Tom Horn could hold a light for.

If only he were here now. From what she knew, he was the same kind of man as her captors, and up until a week ago, the name James Winchester would have curdled her blood and made her skin prickle. But at this moment she would welcome his presence. For the first time in her life she realized that there were times when such a man was needed.

Winchester was, after all, her kin. But if he were here, would that fact even hold any meaning for him?

Julia leaned her head back against the wall. She was only pipe-dreaming. Winchester had no way of knowing of her predicament, and if he knew, he would probably not care. She had despised him as a child, and he had known it.

Hiram brought a tin plate of bacon and beans and set it in her lap. He loosened her hands so she could eat, with a few unneeded caresses here and there, and tiredly, she allowed his hands to roam.

It hardly mattered anymore. There was nothing she

could do but wait. Wait for someone to come . . . or wait for an opportunity to escape, but she knew it was hopeless. If she did get away she had nowhere to go. They would catch her before she could get far.

She ate little of the food offered her. There was no salt on it, and it tasted burned and smoky. Afterward, however, she drifted mercifully off to sleep.

Some time later, she awoke with a start and sat up. The lamp on the table had been extinguished, and the fire had burned low.

Moses and the others were lying on the buffalo robes near the fireplace, all three apparently asleep. One of them was snoring loudly.

It was that that had awakened her.

She noticed that they had neglected to tie her hands back after she had eaten. If she wanted she could easily work them free of the rope now.

But did she want to? She remembered what Moses had told her, about turning her over to Hiram should she try to escape. Would he? She didn't doubt it, for Moses was not that much different from the others. He was a hard man, and he had only protected her thus far because he had plans of his own for her.

Obviously he had ransom in mind, but would he release her if her father paid the ransom? She would be able to identify all of them and bring the law to their hideout.

Suddenly, Julia felt a coldness in the pit of her stomach that she had not felt before. For the first time she was really afraid for her life. It had taken it awhile to soak in. These men were killers. They had proven that when they killed her mother.

Why should they release her after the ransom was

paid? A man who would commit murder would not hesitate to break a promise.

Tears of anger stung her eyes, and Julia began to pull at the ropes that bound her wrists. She obtained slack in one of the loops easily and slipped her hand out, then the other.

She untied her feet and tried to stand up. Tremors coursed through her pain-wracked body, and she bit her lip against crying out.

She looked down at her clothes in the faint light cast by the dying fire. The dress that she had been wearing when she was abducted was practically in tatters. Moses had ripped it off just above the knees so that she might straddle her horse, like a man. Her bare legs below where the dress had been torn off were sun-blistered and scratched. Her hair was stringy and dirty, and she desperately wished for a bath.

The men by the fire continued to snore, and Julia moved silently to the door. The heavy cross-member lay in place in its wooden brackets, and she lifted it gingerly.

Wood creaked against wood, and she caught her breath, looked at the sleeping men.

Hiram stopped snoring suddenly, but none of them moved.

She waited, her back against the wall, praying.

In a moment, the snoring resumed, and she eased the door open and slipped out into the night.

She had no way of knowing the time, but the moon was already down. She presumed it would not be much longer until dawn.

She moved away from the dugout, almost running.

The night air felt good against her flushed face.

Her heart leaped. Maybe she could get away. If the men did not awaken until late this morning, she would be able to put a lot of miles between them. Once she got on her horse she would not stop . . . she would just keep going and going and going . . . until she came to a town or a farmhouse or anyone who would help her.

She stopped and looked around, her heart beating furiously. Where had they left the horses? They were nowhere to be seen in the draw.

She looked back toward the dugout and thought she saw something move. She shook her head to clear it. Just her imagination. There was nothing there . . . nothing at all.

The trees.

She looked up. That's where the horses would be, hidden in the timber.

She scrambled up the cutbank at its lowest point and headed up into the trees on the knoll above the dugout.

In the east, she discerned a faint, gray light beginning to spread. Dawn was only minutes away now. She hadn't much time.

Not far ahead, she saw something move, and then a horse nickered a greeting.

She went to them on the run and caught up the gray she had been riding. She did not see the saddles anywhere, and there was no time to look. She would have to ride bareback.

Julia led the horse down the slope and out of the timber. She caught hold of the mane and started to mount. She looked no longer toward the dugout, and did not see the man coming up behind her.

A strong hand caught her shoulder and jerked her back. She caught a glimpse of Moses' face, his mouth twisted in a snarl.

He slapped her viciously, and lights exploded inside her brain.

She felt herself falling, but she tasted the blood on her lips before the encroaching blackness swallowed her.

Chapter 5

For a long moment Robert Strawbridge did not recognize the man who stood in the open doorway. He was dirty and unshaven and reminded Robert of a buggy whip, dusty and thinned down to a mean edge.

The man's horse, a big gray gelding, was tethered in the yard behind him. A .44 Henry swung loosely in the stranger's left hand.

Recognition came at last, but Strawbridge knew him only from the flat, black eyes that had been his father's.

"Ah, James, it's you," he said finally.

"Hello, Robert," Winchester replied, but there was no smile on his lips or any greeting in his eyes. He had been riding more than a week, practically day and night, with little sleep and less food.

Robert Strawbridge swung the door back. "Come in, won't you?"

Winchester stepped in the door unmindful of the plush carpeting underfoot.

"Can I take your jacket?"

"I'll keep it, thanks."

Strawbridge's smile faded. "Well, can I get you a drink, then?"

"Yeah, somethin' to cut the dust if you've got it." Winchester stood his rifle against the wall and looked around. It was all as he remembered, only a bit fancier. The furniture was new, as was the carpet, and a mahogany rail followed the winding staircase up to the second floor.

Beautifully crafted, glass decanters lined the top of the bar at the back of the big living room, and a glass chandelier hung overhead from one of the huge, wooden beams that lined the cathedral ceiling.

"Have a seat anywhere." Robert Strawbridge walked over to the bar and pulled two glasses from underneath the cabinet. "What'll you have?"

"Whiskey." Winchester stepped over and dropped into a big Morris chair that sat under a painting of wild horses in a meadow.

Strawbridge raised his eyebrows quizzically. "Bourbon?"

"Yeah, that'll do."

The short, bald man brought him three fingers of bourbon in the glass, and Winchester swallowed it, scarcely blinking an eye as the liquor burned its way down his dry throat.

He set the glass on the chairarm. "What can you tell me about the scarfaced man?"

Strawbridge ignored the question. He stared at Winchester openly, as if seeing him for the first time. "I mean no offense," he said finally, "but you look like you've been through hell."

"As near as a man can come to it," Winchester said.

"I came through the badlands."

"Jesus! I've heard it's suicide to go into that country."

"You have to know your way around. Now, what about the scarfaced man?"

Strawbridge shrugged and sat down opposite him. "There were a couple of strangers seen around Council Bluffs a few days before the murder. One of them was a big man with a hideous scar on his face. His description seems to fit the man you're looking for."

"How did you know I was looking for a scarfaced man?"

Strawbridge looked surprised. "Who doesn't know it. You know how word gets around on a man in the west. How do you think all the well known gunfighters and outlaws got their reputations?"

"I'm not an outlaw."

"No, but you must have been holed up in a cave the last five years if you don't know anything of the reputation you're making for yourself."

"You're not the first to tell me that," Winchester said dryly.

"Anyway—" Strawbridge waved the discussion aside— "you're not here to discuss your reputation. I know who you are, and I know what you have become since you left here. So let's just put things in their proper place. For some reason unknown to me, you have no liking for me or this house, and I, on the other hand, do not relish the way you have chosen to make a living.

"However, as much as I hate to admit it, I have a need now for a man of your skills. There has already been a ten-thousand dollar reward posted for the murder of my wife. That should be incentive enough for you, but

I am willing to go a step further. I'm offering you another ten thousand if you will return my daughter to me alive."

"What about the law?" Winchester asked. "Have they not tried?"

Strawbridge nodded. "There were three different posses, and some private detectives, as well. All came back emptyhanded. It rained the day after the murder and washed out any tracks the kidnappers might have left. I've written the Pinkertons, but they don't have an agent free to take the case right away. They said it could be as long as four weeks, but I was afraid that I would not have four weeks. So you see, you are my last resort."

"Have any demands been made?"

"Not yet . . . and that's what's got me worried. I've heard nothing from them, nothing at all."

"What about names? Did the scarfaced man stay at any of the hotels in town?"

"Apparently not. All the strangers in Council Bluffs the day of the murder and a week preceding it have been accounted for. I have questioned all the hotel clerks and seen their registers. No one fitting the scarfaced man's description stayed at any of the hotels, but he was seen on the street and he bought shells for a .45 at the hardware store."

"Tell me about the murder," Winchester said.

Strawbridge's face sickened. The color left his cheeks, and he looked as if Winchester had hit him in the stomach. He stood up. "Come upstairs. I have left everything as it was. I wanted you to have an idea of the kind of man you're going after."

It wasn't necessary, for Winchester had seen many

such men, and knew the stripe well, but he followed Strawbridge upstairs anyway, more out of morbid curiosity than anything else.

Down the hallway there was a door on the right, or at least where a door had once been. The door itself lay on the floor inside the bedroom, and the door casing was splintered off where the hinges had been fastened.

An odor that Winchester knew all too well drifted to his nostrils even before he stepped into the room, the smell of dried blood and death . . . the sickening, sweet smell of rotted flesh.

"I did remove the sheets and pillows from the bed," Strawbridge said, his voice grown husky. "She was raped, you see, and—" he stopped and swallowed, took a deep breath— "and they shot her between the eyes with a .45. It was such a mess that—"

"Yeah, I know," Winchester said, disgustedly. He had a good imagination, for he had seen enough of the same sort of thing, often the result of his own hand.

There remained a great blood stain on the mattress, however, that he did not understand.

"Why all the blood?"

"They cut her throat, too. I don't know which killed her, the knifing or the shooting."

"Christ," Winchester said. Killing he could understand, but the excessive mutilation of a body he could not. It took a goddamned savage to do that.

He pointed to some brown stains on the wall beside the door.

"Tobacco juice," Strawbridge said. "One of them chews tobacco."

"Not much there. A lot of men chew."

"And spit on the walls and bed?"

55

Winchester shrugged. "I'll keep it in mind."

They went back downstairs, and Winchester picked up his rifle. "I'll go into Council Bluffs and do some asking around of my own."

"You're welcome to stay the night here, if you wish."

He shook his head. "No, I've seen all I need to see here. I'll get a room at the hotel. I've got some looking around to do."

"James?"

Strawbridge's tone caused him to turn around.

"I wish you could have known Julia after she grew up. You would have liked her. She turned into quite a lady, very unlike the spoiled brat that you knew. She's a sweet girl, Jim, and a good person."

Winchester was puzzled. "Why are you telling me this?"

"I just pray that you don't let your drive to kill the scarfaced man endanger my daughter's life."

He was thoughtful a moment, then said coldly, "Well, as you said a few minutes ago, I *was* your last resort."

Strawbridge's lips tightened, and he opened the door for him. Winchester went out, shoved his rifle into the saddle boot, and mounted up.

"Do you need any expense money?"

"No, I'll collect when the job's done."

Strawbridge nodded. "Just remember, there'll be twenty-thousand waiting for you if you bring Julia back alive."

Winchester grinned. "You're talking my language." He lifted a hand and rode out north along the river.

It looked as if Robert Strawbridge cared little about avenging his wife's death. He merely wanted his daughter back and could care less whether the kidnappers were caught or not.

But Winchester cared. The only reason he had taken this job was Scarface, and his uncle knew it. He very well had, as Strawbridge pointed out, been the last resort.

He studied the river as he rode along. Something was amiss, but he could not quite put his finger on it. The mutilation of Amanda Strawbridge, the rape. What did it mean?

Why had they taken Julia? Surely not merely to rape and kill her as they had her mother. Winchester could not believe any sane man would kill just for sexual purposes. That was a senseless thing even for an outlaw to do. The penalties for the molestation of women were too harsh. Any man knew that if he were caught he would be hanged on the spot.

It just didn't add up. He had a feeling that this hand was not completely dealt yet. The incentive for the kidnapping was missing.

Why had the posses and the detectives come up empty-handed? It sounded as if the kidnappers had steered clear of the river and the settlements, and had gone into the back country and holed up, possibly somewhere along the Platte.

If that were the case, he had no way of knowing which way to look. There had to be more to go on than that, and he had a feeling there would be more information soon. The kidnappers had not dealt their hole card yet.

Meanwhile, Winchester would have time to scout the country a little. A man never knew what he might stumble across.

As he remembered, Council Bluffs lay only two or three miles from the Strawbridge house, but he came to the outskirts of it sooner than he expected. The town had grown in his absence, swelling out at the sides like a well-fed pup.

It was a thriving river town that depended on the steamboat traffic up and down the Missouri. The waterfronts were a beehive of activity, and the familiar noises of his boyhood came to Winchester faintly on the mid-summer air, the sounds of hammering and building and men shouting.

A steamboat whistled as it came into the wharf, and Winchester felt a longing inside for he knew not what.

Too many dusty miles and too many killings lay behind him. The days of his boyhood spent here in this town seemed an eternity away. He looked around, but saw nothing that he remembered, nothing that rang a familiar note. It was all new, and yet all seen somewhere before, just another town along his way.

He left his horse at the livery on the outskirts of town and walked to what looked like one of the better hotels. He paid the clerk for one night, and a grinning boy about eighteen showed him up the stairs to his room.

At the door, the boy said, "Sir, can I get you anything?" The grin spread further into his freckles.

"As in what?"

"Well . . . a bath, haircut, shave . . . a woman?"

Winchester chuckled. He dug into his shirt pocket and handed the boy twenty dollars. "I'm goin' to sleep first. Tonight I'll take a bath, a shave, and a woman . . . in that order."

"Yes, sir!" The bellboy saluted him smartly and skipped off down the hall.

Winchester tossed his bedroll and personals in the corner, sat down on the edge of the bed and tugged off his boots. Then he propped a chair under the doorknob, slipped the Colt .45 under his pillow, and stretched out on the bed.

The mattress underneath felt like the best thing that had happened to him since Rose McEachen, and he fell asleep almost instantly and slept as if he had been drugged.

He was awakened by a pounding at the door. It was a struggle to open his eyes, and he climbed out of the foggy wells of sleep with difficulty.

"Who the hell is it?"

"Your bath is ready, sir."

Winchester sat up on the side of the bed. He looked toward the window and discovered that it was rapidly getting dark outside.

He pulled on his boots, opened the door, and followed the bellboy downstairs. The bathhouse was a big room at the back of the hotel, and a hot bath had already been prepared for him.

He carried with him his only change of clothes, and took his time with the bath and in shaving the stubble from his face.

Afterward, he took the back alley out of the hotel and located an out of the way cafe on a side street a couple of blocks away. By the time he had eaten and returned to his room, night had fallen completely.

The bellboy was as good as his word. The woman Winchester had been promised was already in his bed. The lamp was burning and she was sitting up, pillows behind her back, reading a newspaper.

She looked up and smiled when he came in. "Hello,"

59

she said, "I'm Flora."

"Hello, Flora." He volunteered nothing else and started shucking his pants and boots.

"You don't have a name, huh?"

He looked at her. The girl was young, in her mid-twenties, and there was a gap in her smile where a tooth had been knocked out, probably by some unappreciative customer. Otherwise, she was moderately pretty. Her hair was silky blond, and she was a little on the skinny side but had large, pendulous breasts.

"You can call me Smith," Winchester said.

"I can't call you James?"

He looked at her.

"When a man like yourself comes to Council Bluffs, Mister Winchester, you'd better wear a sack over your head if you don't want to be noticed. Practically everyone in town knows you're here." The girl touched a hand to her forehead. "Let's see, you arrived at eleven this morning, left your horse at the livery and paid the hostler from a roll of bills as big as your fist. You walked to the hotel, took a room, asked the bellboy for a bath, a shave, and a woman . . . in that order. Shall I go on?"

He threw a boot at the wall in disgust. "No, that'll do."

She blew out the lamp, and Winchester climbed into bed, pulled the woman to him, and absently began to explore her anatomy.

Chapter 6

The woman kept his bed jiggling until after midnight and then, sleepy again and somewhat bored with her, Winchester put her out. It was a standing rule of his never to allow prostitutes to sleep with him after he was finished with their services. He had done so only once, a long time ago, and it had cost him a hundred and fifty dollars and his rifle. He had always been a quick study, though, and he never made the mistake again.

When he awakened the following morning, Winchester repacked his belongings in his bedroom and went back out on the street.

He had slept late, and the town was already stirring. As he went down the boardwalk, he could see no one looking at him, but he could feel their eyes on his back.

He located the hardware store that Strawbridge had spoken of and went inside. There were only a couple of customers in the place, and they departed soon after his entrance.

Winchester picked up two boxes of .45 caliber shells and one box of .44's for the Henry. He laid them on the counter.

"How much?"

The wizened proprietor scratched in his thinning hair nervously as he added with a pencil. He quoted the price, and Winchester paid him, then added two extra dollars on the counter.

"Some information?"

The little man studied him, then looked toward the door. "Depends on what you want to know."

"The day before the Strawbridge woman was murdered you had a customer."

"You mean the man with the scar?"

Winchester nodded. "A scar down the left side of his face?"

The man scratched his head again. "I can't rightly recall. Seems like it might have been the left side, but I wouldn't swear to it."

Winchester's lips tightened. Why didn't anyone ever *look*?

"But he was a big man," the proprietor continued, "big and rawboned. He was mighty dusty, like he'd been a long time on the trail. Had a beard and wore one of those old cavalry pistols . . . you know, the kind they used in the war."

"And he bought shells for the same gun?"

"Yes, sir, .45's, like yourself. Two boxes."

"He was alone?"

"Well, there was a man riding with him, but he didn't come in the store. I saw him standing out there on the walk. He had his back to me, so I didn't get a look at his face, but he was shorter than the man with the scar, but kind of heavy-set, with a beer gut."

"Thanks." Winchester tossed down another dollar and went back out on the walk.

Suddenly, something the storekeeper had said and something he had seen at the Strawbridge house linked together. He was not even sure what he was thinking immediately; it was just some ingrained intuition accumulated with five years of man-hunting that made him stop and turn around.

There, contrasting sharply with the freshly white-washed boards of the store front, between the door and plate glass window, were several splattered, brown splotches.

Tobacco juice.

Robert Strawbridge's words came back to him. *Who spits on walls and beds?*

Winchester stepped back into the street, walked to the livery stable and saddled his horse. He had to talk to Robert Strawbridge again. There were still some missing links, things that would never have been apparent to the untrained eye. Yet such things had been imperative to his survival in the past, and probably would be again.

He rode out of town at midmorning, this time taking the road instead of the river path he had followed before. He did so subconsciously, the caution in his action being simply a part of him. But had he tried to recall it, he would have remembered one of the rules taught him by the Apaches. *A man, especially a white man, is a creature of habit. Never walk the same path twice!*

There were few people on the road, and as he drew

farther from town, he saw no one.

He admonished himself for his growing impatience. He had waited five years for news of the whereabouts of the scarfaced man, he could easily wait a few days more.

He had been too quick to anger when the storekeeper had failed to remember which side of the man's face the scar was on . . . much too quick. He must guard against that. If he did not, it could get him killed when at last he found Scarface.

And if that happened his entire life would have been for nothing. The last five years would be wasted, dust in the wind. The scarfaced man would go forever free, and Winchester's parents would never rest easy in their graves.

Scarface was a dangerous man. Winchester did not know that factually, but his intuition told him that. The man was as elusive as a ghost, and when cornered he would be extremely dangerous. Winchester felt those things in his bones, and he knew that it would take every ounce of the knowledge and skill he possessed to bring the man down.

Suddenly, he was shocked out of his thoughts when the gray stopped abruptly. The horse pricked his ears and snorted uneasily.

Sunlight glinted off something, and Winchester moved instinctively, not a split-second too soon.

A bullet split the air where his head had been, and he hit the ground running, rifle in hand. He made the cover of a copse of pines beside the road, and another bullet from the ambusher sprayed bark from a tree near him.

His horse, who was no stranger to gunfire, did not

run away, but made the cover provided by the pines in two jumps.

Then, just as quickly as it had begun, it seemed to be over. There was no further sound, no movement.

Winchester waited. Someone was still out there, he was sure.

It was quiet. Even the wind was still. Not a bird cried or an insect buzzed.

He peered out from behind a tree as big around as his body. Across the road was another stand of trees, but the rifleman had not been that close. Just ahead, however, on the right side of the road, was a small knoll, barren for the most part, but with a few scrubby oaks and persimmon bushes around the base of it.

It was the only likely spot for a marksman. Winchester was certain the reflection he had seen had been the sun off a rifle barrel.

He studied the knoll closely for movement, but saw nothing. Slowly, he raised the Henry to his shoulder and fired at a rock outcropping on the right side of the knoll.

The shot drew two answers from behind the rocks, but the bullets passed harmlessly into the foliage over his head.

"Fool," he murmured.

Quickly, he slipped back through the trees and began a long circle. The ambusher was not completely inept, for he had selected his position so that the sun would be in Winchester's eyes.

But Winchester did not intend to remain so. He came back out near the road some two hundred yards below the knoll, intending to approach the rifleman from the opposite side.

However, before he could cross the road, he heard the drum of hoofbeats on the other side of the knoll, close by at first, then moving away toward the river.

He heard only one horse. Had there only been one rifleman?

Winchester left nothing to chance. He crossed the road and worked his way up to the back side of the knoll.

No one. The rider had disappeared, obviously running scared after his ambush had failed.

Winchester knelt behind the rocks where the ambusher had hidden and examined the sign. There was an impression in the sand where the gunman had knelt on one knee, more sand dug up behind where his boot toes had dug in, and four empty cartridge casings.

But the last thing he saw made him catch his breath. There, on the rocks and staining a clump of sage close by, was a goodly amount of brown spittle, unmistakably where tobacco juice had been expelled.

He sat back on his heels and calmed himself. It could be . . . but then it just as well might not. As he had said to Robert Strawbridge, a lot of men chewed tobacco.

He stood up, walked around the knoll, and whistled for the gray.

The horse came to him at a trot, and as he came, Winchester heard another rider on the road, headed into town.

He swung up on the gray and started walking him, and as the approaching rider drew near, he recognized Robert Strawbridge, bouncing on the back of a little mare and looking like he had seen a ghost.

The little man drew rein. "Winchester," he said, "I heard shots. Did you see anything?"

"Somebody took a shot at me."

"Who?"

"Damned if I know," Winchester lied. "He got away."

Strawbridge pulled a piece of paper from his pocket. "I was just on my way in to see you. Take a look at this."

Winchester took the paper from him and spread it out. It was an old, worn envelope with a penciled message on the back of it.

The gal is all right. But it will cost you $20,000 to git her back. Put the money in a glass jug and cork it. Put the jug on a rope tied to the dock at Winony. Drop the jug in the river. One week. No tricks.

The note was unsigned, nor was there any mention of where and when Julia would be set free if the demand was met.

"When did you get this?" Winchester said.

"Just a few minutes ago. I heard a knock at the door. I was in my study, and by the time I answered it no one was there. Just this note left by the door."

"Any tracks?"

"I didn't look, but I heard hoofbeats." Strawbridge looked thoughtful. "Are you thinking what I am?"

"That whoever delivered this note was the same one who shot at me?"

Strawbridge nodded.

"Could be."

Strawbridge reached for the ransom note. "I'm going on in to see the sheriff. I—"

"No," Winchester said sharply. "Don't do that."

"What do you mean?"

"Look. You've already been to the law, and they got you exactly nowhere, right?"

"And?"

"I don't want their interference. You hired me for the job, and I don't want the law getting in my way. They have to follow the legalities, rules an' such. I don't. You get my drift?"

Strawbridge sat back in the saddle. "I get it, all right. In other words, you don't want a law man looking over your shoulder when you shoot somebody in the back."

Winchester shrugged. "Call it what you like."

Strawbridge hesitated, then nodded. "All right. I'll play it your way . . . but only to a point. How do you plan to handle it? What about the ransom?"

"Funny about that, isn't it? The same amount of money you offered me to bring the girl back. Where's Wi-nony?"

"Winona," Strawbridge corrected. "It's a little town downriver, thirty or forty miles, or it used to be a town."

"Used to be?"

"Started out as a town, but when Council Bluffs boomed as a river port, everybody moved up here. It's just a river crossing now, mostly deserted. An old man named Bartlett runs a ferry there. You want me to pay the ransom?"

"Maybe. We'll see. Meet me in a week at Winona,

and have the money with you."

"What happens meanwhile?"

Winchester grinned. "I want to have me a talk with a man who likes his tobacco. By the way, how many sets of tracks led away from the house the day of the murder?"

"Three horses, headed southwest."

Winchester looked troubled. He turned the gray and started to head him back off the road, but he drew rein suddenly. "And oh, Robert?"

Strawbridge looked at him.

"I never shot a man in the back in my life," he said softly.

The smaller man paled a little, then nodded. "All right," he said, "all right."

"In a week, then, at Winona." He nudged the gray into a canter, and they left Strawbridge behind on the road and picked up the trail of the tobacco chewer again on the other side of the knoll.

The way Winchester figured, a man who liked his tobacco the way this one did shouldn't be hard to find.

Robert Strawbridge watched his nephew ride away, then turned his mare and started for home. He had wanted to tell him. He had tried, even thought about it while they had talked, but he just could not bring himself to form the words.

What if Winchester became angry when he found out? Lord knew, he would have the right. And he was a dangerous man. Strawbridge would not be surprised if the man killed him on the spot, once he knew the truth.

It had all been Amanda's doing. She had formulated the plan and put it to work. But he had helped. He had gone along with her.

Why? He could not answer that anymore. It had been wrong, terribly wrong, and if he had been the man he should have been it would never have happened.

But then he had never been the man he should be, had he? Strawbridge swore softly to himself. Now that Amanda's support was no longer under him, he could not continue living the lie that had made him what he was. Amanda had suppressed the truth for ten years; she had borne the burden of it. But now she was gone, and it was his burden.

But he could not bear it . . . he would not.

Practically everything he owned rightfully belonged to James Winchester. True, there had not been that much in the beginning, but Winchester's money had been his working capital. Without it he would be nothing.

Why not repay him only the money that had been his in the beginning, the original sum?

The idea was an intriguing one, but if it should work it would be due to Winchester's generosity, and Strawbridge did not think that was likely.

If Winchester chose to take the matter to court, he would be ruined. He would lose everything.

He deserved nothing better than that, Strawbridge admitted. Yet it was a hard pill to swallow. He had had so much for so long that he just could not comprehend losing everything. Losing a part of it he could possibly deal with, but not *all*!

What would he do? Where would he go? He was fifty years old, not so young anymore. If Winchester could be persuaded to take only what his parents had left him, it would not hurt that much. Strawbridge could easily rebuild with what remained.

But would he? Strawbridge doubted it. James Winchester was a vindictive man. He did not accept any wrong done him lying down, and he did not give up easily. Had he not hunted the scarfaced killer the last five years?

But perhaps things were in his favor in that area, Strawbridge considered. It was possible that Winchester had reached the end of his rope. This could be his last manhunt, for those were evil men he sought. And with the death of Winchester, his problems would be over, wouldn't they?

Strawbridge started to chortle, then shook his head suddenly. What was he thinking? What about Julia? If Winchester did not succeed he might never see his daughter alive again.

Strawbridge looked back toward the river, the way his nephew had gone. What had he meant, wanting to talk to a man who liked his tobacco?

Strawbridge kicked the mare back into a trot. There might be a way, after all. There just might be. . . .

Chapter 7

The rain began while she slept, but when Julia awakened she heard the sounds of it outside the dugout, and the rush of the wind.

She shivered under the smelly buffalo robe as she sat up and looked around. It was night, and she was alone again, as she had been a good part of the time the last several days. The fire had burned low, but it was not cold inside the dugout, and Julia was thankful that at least she was dry. Things could be much worse.

She had not been bothered, and seldom spoken to, the last three days. Moses had sent the tobacco chewer, Hiram, away. For what purpose she did not know, but she had pieced a little of it together. Moses had worked painstakingly over a piece of paper one morning, and when he was finished with it, all three men had gone outside the door. She had heard Hiram complaining loudly, but afterward he had gone away, and no mention from the others as to where.

Thunder rumbled ominously, shook the earth under her, and Julia clutched the robe tighter around her neck. Her hands and feet were still tied, and the door, she knew, was locked from the outside. She had already tried it.

They did not trust her in the least. She had already proven to be an innovative escapist, and since the last time they had given her fewer opportunities.

She touched her still tender lip, remembering. Moses, she supposed, was the best of a bad lot, but given the right circumstances he had proven that he had little regard for womanhood, either.

The nondescript man called Pete she had not figured out yet. He seemed to be extremely withdrawn, never spoke unless Moses addressed him first, and never spoke to her at all. He wore old, faded overalls, block-toed brogans, and a slouch hat. Actually, he looked like a farmer, except for one thing . . . the tied down gun on his right hip. He wore the gun swung low for a fast draw, and its wooden grips were worn smooth from much use.

The storm outside increased in intensity, and just when it seemed to be at its peak, she heard noises outside.

The door swung open, emitting a gust of wind and rain, and two slicker-draped figures stamped in and barred the door behind them.

"Where the hell can he be?" she heard Moses say, under his breath.

Pete did not answer, but went to the fire and stirred it back to life, laid on more wood.

Julia pretended to be asleep in case the men should talk among themselves. But she did not expect it.

Moses rarely attempted to converse with the other man, for Pete usually only responded with a grunt, a yeah, or a maybe.

What was he doing here with the likes of Moses and Hiram? At the scene of the murder, Pete had taken no part in either the raping or the killing. But neither had he tried to stop it; he had merely looked on, unflinching. He, too, was a hard man, but not of the same caliber as the others. Once, when Julia had caught him looking at her, she thought she had detected compassion in his eyes. But she could have been wrong. It was probably just wishful thinking.

Suddenly, Moses walked over and gave her legs a kick, and Julia sat up, startled.

"Can you cook?" he demanded.

She opened her mouth to speak, but on second thought closed it and shook her head defiantly.

"Then you best start learnin'." He knelt and began to untie her hands and feet.

"I'll do no such thing," she said heatedly. "I'm your captive, and you can prevent me from escaping, but you can't force me to cook for you. I won't."

Moses chuckled. "Is that right?"

"Certainly. What will you do now, shoot me like my mother?"

"Not likely. You're worth too much alive. But you do want to eat, don't you?"

She was silent then. What did he mean?

"It's like this, see," he went on. "Hiram was our best cook, and he's gone. Pete an' me, we can't even boil water without burnin' it, can we, Pete?"

Pete continued to nourish the fire. He didn't look up at the mention of his name, nor bother to agree.

"So," Moses said, "whenever you get hungry enough you'll roust your butt up and get to fixin'. And you best fix enough for all three of us."

"Or what?"

"Or I'll give you an upper lip to match the lower one," he said thinly.

Julia touched her puffy lip and believed him. He would do it, she knew. Probably the only thing she had learned of Moses so far was that he did not mince words.

She got up and started for the fire, but found it an arduous chore. She had not been on her feet in three days, and she ached from head to toe.

She located the utensils and the tins of beef and beans and set about stirring up the usual fare.

Moses went to where he had left his slicker, brought back a paper-wrapped package and held it out to her. "Coffee," he said.

Julia took the package without asking where he had come by it. Stolen it, she presumed. Surely they had not dared show their faces back in Council Bluffs.

The two men sat down and watched her cook. She looked at them out of the corner of her eye. "Have you ever," she asked, "heard of a man named Winchester?"

Moses stared at her. "Who ain't?"

She shrugged indifferently. "Just wondered if you knew him."

A pregnant silence ensued, and Julia felt the tension mount in the men behind her. It was the effect she wanted. It was just an idea, but what other hope did she have?

"What the hell about Winchester?" Moses demanded finally.

"Just that he's my cousin . . . first cousin. And," she lied, "we were very close once, when we were growing up, and you can bet he'll be coming for me. I wouldn't give a plugged nickel for either one of your hides at this minute."

Moses' eyes bugged, and he paled a little. "You're lying."

Julia shrugged. "It doesn't matter. I won't argue with you. You'll find out soon enough."

"The last I heard of Winchester," Pete said suddenly, "he was in Deadwood. Killed a man up there three, four weeks ago."

"Deadwood," Moses said, almost to himself, "that ain't far as the crow files."

"Not near far enough," Pete agreed.

"You scared, Pete?"

"No, just cautious. He's good with a gun . . . damn good. I saw him once."

"So are you. Think you can take him?"

Pete shrugged. "I've got no hankerin' to find out. I don't push my luck. She could be lying, anyway."

Julia cast a candid look at Moses again. He looked troubled, deep in thought.

"Well," he said, "we'll see it through. We'll go to Winona and collect the money, and then clear the hell out."

"What if Strawbridge don't pay?"

"We'll see about that when the time comes."

"That scarfaced man that Winchester searches for," Julia put in, "is that you, Moses?"

"Shut the hell up and cook!"

She drew back from his swift anger. Was it true? Was he the fabled Scarface? He certainly looked the part. She had not thought of it before, but if anyone had actually seen these men around Council Bluffs, it was possible that James Winchester *could* be on their trail. Surely her father would have contacted him.

Her thoughts began to race again as her hopes rose. Could the idea that had begun as a pipe dream actually be true? It was still a long shot, and she had nothing to really support it except her own conjuring. But it was worth thinking about. After all, how many hopes did she have of coming out of this alive?

She served up the food on tin plates and said nothing more. Only time would tell, and that she had plenty of.

Fifty miles to the east a lone rider put his horse to a hard canter through the sandy bottoms that sided the river. The horse was tired and well-lathered, and the man who rode him had a worried look on his face.

Dawn had broken rosy in the east with the passing of the rain, and Hiram Johnson, the tobacco chewer, knew he was in trouble. He had played hell in shooting that Winchester. He should have known that men of his stripe did not die that easily. But the opportunity had afforded itself, and it had been a spur-of-the-moment decision.

He had learned from a passer-by that Jim Winchester had arrived in Council Bluffs, and though Hiram was not the brightest of men, he had reasoned that the bounty hunter could be there for no reason other than tracking them. Winchester's reputation was well known in Hiram's circles, and when he had spied the gray horse on the river road, he had known it was the bounty man.

An instant of false intelligence had flickered in Hiram's brain when he saw the gray horse. Why not drop Winchester, here and now, and put an end to the menace before it even started? It would be so simple. . . .

But it had not been. Hiram had figured a well-placed bullet in the spine and this legend called Winchester would die as easily as any man. And it might have been so. Hiram would never know, for he had missed his shot, missed it clean. The gray horse had alerted the bounty man, and he had missed.

He knew Winchester was behind him now; he felt it in his bones, and he was scared. He did not dare return to Moses and the others. Winchester would follow him, and besides that, Moses would kill him if he learned what he had done.

Hiram drew his horse up in a copse of timber and dismounted, giving the horse a breather he could ill afford. From his plug he cut another chew of tobacco and slipped it in his mouth.

A shiver went through him. Winchester was back there, all right, coming. He had been unable to shake him in two days, and he had not been able to bring himself to lay another ambush. The first one had failed, and Winchester would be on the lookout for it now.

He wallowed the tobacco in his jaw, spat a stream of dark brown juice against the slick bark of a gum tree, and watched it trickle down. He smiled suddenly as another infrequent flicker occurred in his somewhat twisted mind.

He had friends along the river. Some he had not seen in a while, but he saw no reason why they would not still be there.

He smiled again and spat another stream of juice. That was it, he would simply disappear, right into thin air. And the place he was going, there would be no tracks for Winchester to follow.

Moses and the others would wonder what had happened to him, but they would be proud when they found out what he had done. He, Hiram Johnson, had escaped the great James Winchester.

He chuckled aloud, liking the idea. He could just see Winchester's face when he came to the place where the trail ended, stopped as if he had sprouted wings and flown like a bird.

He mounted up. First he must find the place, and as he remembered, it was not far from here.

He laughed again at his cunning, and spurred his horse into a run.

Chapter 8

After Winchester left Robert Strawbridge behind on the road, he trailed the tobacco chewer to a point several miles south of Council Bluffs. There, the man took the road again, and Winchester lost his trail amid the confusion of tracks.

After some lengthy canvassing, however, he discovered where the man had left the road again and headed into the nearby hills. The trail led Winchester to a cold camp some five miles from town, well concealed in the timber and watered by a spring-fed stream.

From the sign, a group of men had camped there several days. A lean-to had been hastily erected, and a great deal of wood burned in the campfire. A rusted out coffee pot had been abandoned, and a tin plate. Unmistakably, the tobacco chewer had been there, and at least two others. There was evidence of a lot of lounging around by the men . . . waiting.

Waiting for what? For Strawbridge to leave the

house, perhaps? Had kidnapping been their principal objective, and the murder of Amanda Strawbridge only incidental?

It seemed to fit. Only two men had been sighted in Council Bluffs, so the third must have been watching the Strawbridge house, waiting for the right opportunity.

Winchester would bet his last dollar that if he returned to the Strawbridge house, he would find a place where someone had lain in hiding, watching the house. But there was no need for it.

He continued to follow the tobacco chewer south, for two days, always paralleling the river, sometimes moving close to the banks of the water, and sometimes farther out into the outlying hills.

It was an erratic pattern that puzzled Winchester, but not a difficult trail to follow. Everywhere he rode the man left a trail of tobacco spittle, on trees, on the ground, apparently any direction his head was turned when the need came.

There was just one thing that continued to puzzle Winchester, a piece of the jigsaw that did not fit.

Who was that third man? Unlike the other two, Scarface and the tobacco chewer, he had kept out of sight. It did not seem like anything really, and it probably wasn't, but it worried him, still. The man had displayed a caution that the others lacked. It could mean nothing at all, but it could also mean that he was the most dangerous man among them. It might be a thing to remember when the showdown came.

In the late evening of the second day, Winchester pulled in the gray and stopped to study the trail. He had just ridden through a heavily wooded draw and picked up the trail again in the sand on the other side. The river was scarcely a hundred yards away, for he could hear the lap of the water against the banks.

Something was wrong with the trail. Where it left the timber and began anew in the sand, the horse had been in a dead-out run.

Why? The tracks were hours old. The tobacco chewer could not possibly have sighted him in pursuit, but what else could have prompted him to run his horse?

It must be a trick, but of what sort?

Winchester touched his heels to the gray and continued to follow the tracks. About a mile farther on, he had his answer. The horse stopped running, turned around in his tracks a few times, then began to wander aimlessly, stopping frequently to graze.

The horse was riderless. Winchester turned back, rode back to the timber where the horse had first begun running. He felt somewhat sheepish, for he had been fooled briefly. It had been a good trick, but an old one, much overused. He had seen it a number of times and should have detected it sooner.

The tobacco chewer had dismounted in the edge of the timber, slapped his horse into a run, perhaps firing a shot to keep him going.

Winchester backtracked through the trees, scanned the area for any sign of a man on foot. The process was more painstaking and time-consuming than following a mounted rider.

He canvassed the area once, then again, thoroughly, but found nothing . . . nothing at all.

He swore and rode around the perimeter of the

woods, then a larger circle farther out.

Still nothing.

In five years of manhunting, Winchester had never seen anything quite like it. It was as if the man had disappeared into thin air.

He dismounted from the gray and let him blow. How could a man disappear without a trace, and especially a man who had spat tobacco juice from Council Bluffs halfway to Winona?

It just didn't add up. Was the man a master trickster, and the tobacco juice trail a part of the trick? Was he a decoy to get Winchester out of the way? The man had, after all, fired at him and missed an easy shot clean, then took off down the river leaving a trail a ten-year old could have followed.

Winchester cursed the thought bitterly, but turned his attention back to the immediate problem. How did a man walk on air, or on water?

Water.

He looked toward the river. At one point between the river and the timber was a stretch of rocky, shale-covered ground that a man would leave little sign on.

If the tobacco chewer had wrapped his boots with cloth and walked carefully . . .

He scanned the area but found no trace of anyone's passing. He moved on toward the river bank and stood there a moment, watched the roll of the muddy water contemplatively.

He was about to turn away when something caught his eye. Protruding from the riverbank directly below him was the root of a tree whose trunk had long since been swept away by flood. A six inch strip of bark had been peeled from the root just above the waterline, possibly by a rope.

On closer inspection, he found an indentation in the riverbank where something had bumped it hard.

Had the tobacco chewer been picked up by a boat? It was possible, but such sign on the riverbank was not uncommon. Besides the steamboat traffic, there were countless skiffs and mackinaws on the Missouri. River pirates were common. The boat that had been tied up here could have been anyone's.

Winchester looked up and down the river but saw no approaching vessels. He whistled for the gray, mounted up, and continued downstream. He stayed a hundred yards or more away from the riverbank but always in sight of the water.

Presently he heard the approach of a sidewheeler and drew the gray up in a stand of water oak, holding him still until the boat churned past.

A few minutes later a mackinaw, manned by half-dozen men, floated downstream, and again he stopped lest he draw attention.

It was almost nightfall when he spotted the boat moored to the bank. Three-hundred yards upstream of the vessel he stopped, tied his horse behind some foliage, and concealed himself behind a willow and the coming night.

The boat was an old, remodeled keelboat with a ragged sail and a dilapidated hull. A large cabin occupied half the deck. It was the type of craft preferred by the river rats, people who lived and worked, or pirated, on the water.

Winchester watched the boat for a half-hour, but he saw nothing. No one showed their face on deck, and there was no sound from the cabin.

At last, after full darkness had fallen, a light appeared within the cabin, and a shadowy figure came on deck and lighted the lantern that hung from the rudder, a warning to other boats that might venture near in the darkness.

Winchester began to work his way closer to the keelboat. He stopped finally behind a small embankment, fifty yards away. He could hear voices now, men's voices, more than one, and then the whiskey laugh of a woman.

Kneeling on his toes, Winchester leaned on his rifle and waited, biding his time until the moon was high. The light would be good enough for shooting then, should there be any.

Three men came out of the cabin, all big men, one with a paunch that hung over his belt. That one, Winchester thought, could be his man.

Two of them talked and laughed drunkenly while the man with the paunch urinated into the river, and as he relieved himself, he twisted his head suddenly and spat.

One of the others tipped a bottle to his mouth, then handed it to the man with the paunch.

The moon was high, and the muddy river gleamed dully, menacingly, under the white light. The keelboat had drifted broadside against the bank, its deck only a long step from shore.

The three men had their backs to him, and Winchester made his move, stepped lightly to the embankment, jumped, and landed lightly on the balls of his feet aboard the keelboat.

"Good evening, gentlemen."

The three turned around and stared at him stupidly. One was very drunk, another almost as bad, but Winchester was not sure of the condition of the tobacco chewer. Appearances were sometimes deceiving.

He covered them casually with his rifle, and they lifted their hands. Only the tobacco chewer was armed, but he held himself very still, hands away from his gun.

"Who the hell are you?" the larger of the other two demanded.

"Doesn't matter," Winchester said. "I've got no truck with you boys. It's that one—" he indicated the man with the paunch— "that I want to talk to."

"You talk to him, you talk to us," the drunk blustered. "Hiram's our frien'."

Winchester shrugged. "So be it. If you want dealt into the hand I'll be glad to oblige. You—" he pointed to the tobacco chewer— "get over against the rudder."

Hiram did so meekly, staggered a little as he went.

"You two," he said to the others, "jump in the river."

"Jesus, mister, I can't swim!"

"High time you learned, then. Jump!" He levered a shot at their feet that sent up a shower of splinters, and the two men scrambled for the side of the boat and went over it into the water.

A head bobbed up a few yards downstream, but no sign of the other one. Winchester looked again at the side of the boat and saw a set of white-knuckled fingers gripping the top rail.

He covered the tobacco chewer with the rifle, drew his Colt and fired at the hand.

Blood and bone sprayed out over the water, followed by a strangled scream and some furious splashing as the non-swimmer fought the water.

The man they had called Hiram swallowed hard. "You're Winchester, ain't you?"

"You know me?"

"You're the only bastard I know would do a thing like that."

Winchester smiled. "Am I? What about what you and your buddies did to Amanda Strawbridge?"

Hiram paled a little, his throat worked. "I don't know what you're talkin' about."

"Well, I'm not interested in her, anyway. Tell me about Julia Strawbridge. Where is she?"

"I don't know any Julia, either."

Winchester swiveled the Colt and fired, and where Hiram's hands had been gripping the side of the boat, a finger disintegrated and the stump spewed blood.

Hiram dropped to his knees, clutched the mangled hand, agony etched in every line of his face. His mouth opened to scream, but he made no sound.

"You've got nine more of 'em," Winchester said. "Start talking."

No sooner were the words out of his mouth than Winchester saw a fleeting shadow behind him and to his left. He started to turn . . . too late. There was only a flash across his conscious mind before he was hit.

A woman's laugh . . . he had forgotten the woman.

Something exploded viciously along the side of his head, and he saw a million brilliant lights and felt himself falling. He landed with arms draped across

88

the railing of the boat, and someone grabbed his legs and rolled him into the river.

The shock of the icy water brought semi-consciousness. Winchester felt himself strangling, choking. He tried to breathe and sucked in only water.

He knew he was drowning but tried not to panic. He could swim . . . he must not fight the water . . . kick and pull, kick and pull.

After a long half-minute that could have been an eternity, he surfaced and sucked for air. His lungs burned with suffocation, and a red mist obscured his vision.

Somewhere far away he heard the report of a rifle, and water sprayed him. Another shot followed and more spray. His limbs were growing numb, and he felt himself sinking again. He tried once more not to panic but could not prevent it.

He clawed desperately at his slipping grasp of the surface and steadily lost the battle. It was like quicksand; the harder he fought the faster he sank.

Then, just as he struggled to breathe and sucked in more water, his hand brushed something hard and solid. He struggled to reach it, but the object was covered with slime and slipped away from him.

He kicked and reached for it again, this time catching the branch of what felt like a deadfall, a chunk of driftwood.

He pulled it to him and wrapped his arms around the trunk of it. It was what a boatman would have called a snag, a piece of a tree about four feet long and a foot and a half in diameter. There were a couple of protruding limbs, one of which he had caught hold of. The snag was covered with a slick, brownish green slime.

He hung his chin over one of the limbs, just above the water line, and tried to breathe. He could not, for he had already taken in too much water.

The red mist in front of his eyes turned black, and he lost consciousness, but dimly, he heard the report of the rifle.

Something whacked the side of his head like a seasoned axe handle, and he knew nothing more. Blood ran freely from his neck and blended with the muddy water, leaving a dissipating trail behind him that could be followed in the moonlight.

He drifted out of range of the keelboat, and there were no more shots.

The night drifted by unnoticed by Winchester as he moved slowly down the river. The driftwood maintained a course near the bank, and at some time he could not remember, Winchester threw a leg over the trunk of it so he would not lose his hold.

At some point he thought he was dreaming, but it was not a dream at all, rather a nightmare. First came the diabolical Scarface, head thrown back and spewing laughter, and when the laughter finally ended all that remained in its place was a deathshead. The head was a hideous, grinning thing which spat tobacco juice. Its hollow eyes mocked him, taunted him, then started to become the devilish side of people that he knew. It was the girl in the hotel room in Council Bluffs, grinning at him with a missing tooth, saying, "when a man like you comes to town . . . you better wear a sack over your head."

Winchester saw himself with that sack over his head, and with a noose around his neck, standing on the gallows. Below him were a number of faces that had come to watch him hang. There was his dead mother, disappointment in her eyes, and Robert Strawbridge, and Rose McEachen, crying for him. And in the distance, a gigantic, scarred head grinned at him from the sky, bellowing laughter.

Consciousness evaded him, and the delirious dreams persisted. At dawn the following morning the deadfall lodged for an hour or more against the bank but was finally washed free and moved on down the river.

He did not know how many hours passed, but when he opened his eyes for the first time it was only to the muddy water drifting by a few inches from his face. His head pounded like a drum in a Fourth of July parade.

He raised his fingers to the side of his face and they came away sticky with blood. The hand dropped back into the water, and he remained motionless. His body was numb with cold and pain.

Only a few minutes of consciousness was all that he could bear. He welcomed the warm cloud of blackness again.

About midmorning the deadfall lodged against the river bank again, and this time it stayed there, water lapping over the trunk of it and splashing on the unconscious man's legs.

A mile downriver, a steamboat whistled its approach, but Winchester did not lift his head.

Chapter 9

He awoke in a warm, dark place. It felt like a bed he was lying on, a feather mattress. But how could that be? It seemed only moments ago that he had looked at the river moving past his face.

A fire burned nearby. He could see the flicker of it on the board ceiling overhead and hear the pop and crackle. It was very warm, and he was tucked in snugly with a blanket.

He tried to turn his head to look around but the movement caused such a throbbing in his brain that he abandoned the idea. He lifted a hand to his head and discovered that it was wrapped in a cloth bandage.

Then he remembered. The rifle shots. He had taken a ricochet after catching onto the driftwood. But how had he arrived at this place? He did not remember getting out of the river. Had someone pulled him out, or did he have amnesia?

Winchester closed his eyes again and tried to think.

How long had he been here? Was he a captive, or had a stranger taken him in?

He opened his eyes suddenly and saw a movement near his bed. A slim figure stood at his side a moment and looked down at him. In the dim but dancing firelight he recognized a girl in a flower-patterned shift. Other than that, all he could discern was that she had long, dark hair and big, staring eyes.

Without speaking, she flipped back the blankets and crawled into the bed beside him. She pressed against him, timid but warm, and the sweet, woman smell of her teased Winchester's nostrils.

He tried to speak but found his throat was too dry. He closed his mouth and swallowed, afraid to move his head for the frightful pounding.

A hand worked its way slowly across his chest, down his abdomen and lower stomach, and finally sought his crotch.

He caught his breath, and she began to massage him gently.

"Who—" he managed at last— "are you?"

The massage stopped, and the girl lay still, breathed heavily against his shoulder, but she did not speak.

After a moment, she continued her advances, and the reaction in him was swift and purely natural. What would any other man do?

The pounding in Winchester's head had little effect on his other organs. His arousal was great, and the slender stranger in his bed had asked for nothing more.

She slipped out of the thin shift without uncovering herself, and mounted him agilely, like a cat. Her small breasts were hard against his chest and her mouth was open, inviting plunder.

When she had taken him into her, her long, contented sigh told him everything. She proceeded quickly to her goal, as if she were afraid of being caught, like the farmer's daughter in the hayloft. With small, animal grunts of pleasure she satisfied herself, then him.

Afterward, as silently as she had entered the bed, she left, slipped back into her shift and disappeared from the room.

Winchester lay there and stared, her kiss still on his lips, somewhat confused. What had all that been about? He shrugged and tried to put it out of his mind. He supposed that she felt as he always had: If you feel the need, scratch.

The excitement left him finally and he slept again, this time dreaming his old dream of the scarfaced man, but now he took satisfaction in knowing that Scarface was probably not far away. He was on his trail this time; he had talked to a man who had actually seen him. Soon the quest would be over. He could almost feel it. He could feel the buck of the Colt in his fist and see the gush of blood from the ragged hole in Scarface's forehead. The gun would buck again and another hole would appear, this one in the heart . . . and then another and another. Scarface would die at his feet, and the dreams would end. He would be tormented no more, and his dear father and mother would smile and rest in peace.

Winchester awoke the following morning with a smile on his lips, but whether from the dream or his night visitor he was not sure.

He sat up slowly and found that his pounding headache had partially subsided, but his head still felt like a huge, rotten melon that had popped open from overripeness.

He found his clothes beside the bed and dressed. His rifle was gone, he knew, and his holster was lying beside his clothes. It, too, was empty.

He swore softly. He had lost both his guns, and he had favored that Colt. It would take a long time to replace it. The only weapon in his possession now was the knife that had been strapped in his boot, but in the right hands a knife was not to be taken lightly. This one was razor sharp. Winchester could, and had on occasion, shaved with it.

The room that he had been in was part of a two-roomed log cabin, chinked tight against the cold and tidy inside, revealing a woman's touch.

He went to the door and looked out. Only a couple of hundred yards away lay the river, so he could not be far from the keelboat, unless they had fled, but he did not think that likely. They were probably still holding their bellies, laughing at him.

It had been his own fault. He was slipping; he could think of no excuse why he had forgotten that woman in the cabin. In the past, it had been his attention to detail that had saved him in many situations. And if he continued in the way of the past several days, it would be his inattention that would get him killed.

Down by the river, an old man with a gray beard was hauling on a rope attached to a flat-bottomed ferry, trying to pull it to the bank.

Winchester walked down to the riverbank and

caught hold of the rope behind the old man.

They hauled the ferry to shore and tied it fast to the makeshift dock there.

The old man turned his whiskered visage around to look Winchester over. He was old and stooped, but there was that unmistakable, flinty look in his eyes that spoke of the he-wolf.

"Come around finally, did ye?"

Winchester nodded. "How long have I been out?"

"A few hours. I dragged you out of the river late yesterday. You took a nasty lick on the head—lost some blood. Looked to me like a ricochet. A clean bullet don't leave a gash like that."

"I had a run-in with some river pirates."

The old man nodded, satisfied with the answer. He stuck out a horny hand. "Name's Bartlett, Amos Bartlett."

Winchester accepted the hand. "Jim Winchester."

"Heerd of ye."

"This is Winona?"

"What's left of her. Nobody here now but me an' the wife. I make a fair living ferryin' folks over to Nebrasky and Kansas, but nothin' to brag on. Business is slow. Everybody else picked up and moved to Council Bluffs and St. Joe. The town—" he pointed out beyond the cabin that lay nearest the river—"was over there, but I've burned most of the buildings for firewood the last three, four years. Nobody was ever comin' back, anyhow."

They walked back toward the cabin.

"I've been looking for three men," Winchester said. "One's got a scar on his face, a bad one, another's got a pot gut and chews a lot of tobacco."

Bartlett shook his head. "I ain't laid eyes on a soul but you in four, five days. What you want 'em for?"

"They murdered a woman in Council Bluffs and kidnapped another."

"Shit," Bartlett said, disgustedly, "what's the world a-comin' to? I knew Jesse James personal, a few years back, and the Younger brothers, too. They would never have done a thing like that, and would have shot the men that did as quick as you or I. There ain't no more *real* outlaws, just a bunch of back-shooters and women-killers."

They stopped in front of the cabin, and suddenly, over the old man's shoulder, Winchester saw the girl standing in the doorway of the cabin. She looked at him momentarily, then cast her eyes shyly to the ground.

Bartlett turned around and saw her. "This here," he said, "is my wife, Little Swallow."

He nodded at the slender Indian girl. "Pleased to make your acquaintance, ma'am."

She nodded and smiled, revealed a mouthful of perfect, white teeth.

"She's Mandan," Bartlett stated, and stared at Winchester defiantly, as if expecting a derogatory comment.

Winchester did not make one. He just smiled at the girl over Bartlett's shoulder and said, "And she's a mighty pretty hostess, too. I can't remember better hospitality anywhere."

Bartlett beamed. "Yessiree-bob, she's a fine girl. No white woman could hold her a light. I know, 'cause I was married to a white woman, once. Nothing but bitch, bitch and gripe, gripe, buy me this an' buy me that, do this an' do that. These Indian gals, now they know how to treat a man. They keep their mouths shet and do what they're told. Yessiree, they know what to do."

"I'll bet they do," Winchester said, smiling at Little Swallow, "I'll just bet they do."

Little Swallow disappeared back into the house with a giggle.

He turned back to Bartlett. "I've got some business to attend to back up the river. Might you have a horse I could borrow for a couple of hours, or a gun?"

"Nary a horse. I've got one old mule but she won't ride nobody but me. I've owned horses on top of horses in my time and every one come up stole, sooner or later. This mule, though, I've kept for five years. Anybody but me tries to git on her back and they'd get pitched clean acrost the river."

"What about a gun?"

"All I've got is one ol' scatter-gun, and she stays here with me, too. I reckon you can appreciate that."

Winchester nodded. "Guess I'll have to walk it, then."

"Goin' after them pirates?"

"Yeah, but I'll be back in a few hours, maybe. I'm expecting someone. A man named Strawbridge is supposed to meet me here. If he shows up while I'm gone, you tell him I'll be back directly."

He walked off toward the river, and Bartlett called after him, "You have a care, young'un. Some of them river rats is salty customers."

Winchester lifted a hand in acknowledgment and kept walking. Something in the back of his mind was telling him that this was another damn fool thing he was doing, but he had a score to settle with those river pirates.

They would still be there, drunk probably, chortling over what they had done to him. But they wouldn't have the chance again. This time he would not be so hasty. There were some forgotten skills he possessed that needed sharpening, things taught him by the Apache.

There were three men on board that keelboat, three men and a woman. This time he would not forget that woman, for she was hell on wheels with a whiskey bottle. And when he had disposed of her and the two others, there was the tobacco chewer.

The tobacco chewer . . . the only stop between Scarface and himself. It was so close that he could taste it, only hours away now. He remembered his dream, the bucking Colt in his hand, the bullets that would smash the teeth out of Scarface's grinning head.

How far down the river he had drifted Winchester did not know, but he suspected the keelboat had only been a few miles from Winona.

He walked for an hour or more, until exhaustion forced him to stop and rest. He wondered suddenly how long it had been since he had eaten, but he could not remember. It was no wonder that his legs were going weak under him.

Again he admonished himself. So eager was he in his pursuit of the Scarface that he was forgetting even to eat. How did he expect to have the strength he would need to bring the man down?

He sat down under a willow tree beside the river, but only for a few minutes, then he got up and stumbled on as the sun climbed toward its noonday position.

His eyes constantly searched the river, but he saw nothing of the keelboat and had a scary thought. What if they had fled, moved farther downriver during the night? They could have drifted past him while he was lying unconscious on the chunk of driftwood.

Winchester swore softly. It did not matter where they had gone. He would find them again if it took a week.

About midafternoon he stopped for a breather, and some distance away, he thought he heard the click of a hoof on rock.

He stood up and listened, and a moment later he heard it again, closer now. He whistled softly, just loud enough to carry on the still air.

The drum of hoofbeats gained momentum, and over the knoll fifty yards ahead a horse came into view. It was the gray gelding, still saddled.

The horse came to him at a canter, breaking stride only a few feet away and stopping on his front feet, legs stiff. He nickered and kicked up his heels.

A lump rose in Winchester's throat, and he laughed aloud and threw an arm around the horse's neck. "Good boy," he said. "I might've known you was looking for me. Good ol' gray."

The horses' feet were muddy, and his tail was full of burrs. The saddle had slipped a little and the rifle boot was empty, Winchester's bedroll gone. He presumed someone had caught the horse and gone through his belongings. The gray had probably broken and run from them, or they would have taken the

101

saddle.

He rubbed the horse down a little with his hands, tightened the saddle, and mounted. He put the gray to a trot along the river bank.

Within minutes after the gray had found him, Winchester approached some familiar ground and spotted the keelboat, still moored to the bank in the same place it had been before.

He dismounted on the knoll above the boat and bellied down in some bunch grass to await the coming night.

Chapter 10

As darkness fell over the river there was no sound but the cicadas chirping and the lap of the muddy water as it ate away at the banks.

Shortly after nightfall someone came on the keelboat's deck and lighted the warning lantern, then disappeared back into the cabin. From his vantage point on the knoll, Winchester could hear the low murmur of voices on the still, night air, and the occasional laugh of the woman.

He waited, patience almost an inbred part of his existence. He had bungled this job once. He would not do so again. Reaching into his boot, he pulled out his knife and tested its edge. It was a heavy-handled blade, not made for throwing, but for close work only. It was about nine inches long overall, bone-handled, and razor sharp.

The knife was not an unfamiliar weapon to Winchester. When he had lived among the Apache, it had been the only thing that stood between himself and death many times. If a man knew how to use a knife, and when, it was often more effective than a gun, for it did its work quietly when there was a need for quiet and stealth . . . like tonight.

When the time was right, just before the moon began to wane, Winchester left the bunch grass on the knoll and moved down alongside the river, about fifty yards above the keelboat.

He slid into the water, and the bite of it took his breath for a moment. His feet groped downward but did not find the bottom, and he was forced to swim. He swung his arms from side to side in a semi-circle, merely floating, letting the current push him along.

He stayed close to the bank, wanting the cover of the shadow cast by it, and within minutes he had drifted alongside the keelboat. He took a breath and went under the water, swam under the rough logs of the boat, and surfaced on the other side.

He caught hold of the lower railing, near the wall of the cabin, and pulled himself onto the deck. He flattened out against the wall of the cabin, breathing heavily from exertion and the shock of the cold water. His hair and clothes dripped puddles around him.

Inside the cabin, the voices were loud and raucous. From the sounds of them, they were drinking again. He singled out the whiskey laugh of the woman and at least two other voices.

He retrieved his knife from the sheath in his boot and waited beside the door. He shivered a little as the night breeze fanned his wet clothes. He was not comfortable, but he would wait until someone came out of the cabin, or until they all slept.

The moon went down, and he stood very still. His

clothes stopped dripping finally and began to dry on his body.

A half-hour passed . . . then an hour.

At last Winchester heard footsteps amid all the drunken talking and laughing. The steps came toward the door and the latch moved.

He stiffened and gripped the knife.

The door opened, and one of the two men stumbled out. He turned half-around as he closed the door behind him, and Winchester held his breath.

Not this close to the door . . .

Drunk, the man did not see him, and he turned and staggered on across the deck to the railing where he undid his pants and began to relieve himself into the river.

Winchester moved, silently even in his boots. He slipped an arm around the man's neck and jerked, cutting off any sound. His right hand held the knife, and he slipped it around the man and stabbed viciously, upward and inward, at a sharp angle just inside the ribcage.

A gush of warm blood greased Winchester's hand as he withdrew the blade. The knife had pierced the heart. The big man emitted a strangled gasp, went slack in Winchester's arm, dying almost instantly.

He let him fall to the deck, then hooked a foot under the corpse's midriff and toed him into the river. There was a small splash, and the body drifted downstream, turned lazily around and around with the current.

No longer than the man had lain on the deck, he had gushed out an enormous puddle of blood. Winchester dragged a tarpaulin over it and retreated again

105

to the wall of the cabin.

The first one had been the larger of the two men. That meant that the smaller man, the one who couldn't swim, was still inside along with the woman and, Winchester hoped, the tobacco chewer. But he had not heard the latter speak . . . only the woman and the man who couldn't swim.

Maybe he had gotten drunk and passed out. But if he wasn't in the cabin, where was he?

Winchester looked around, suddenly nervous. He did not like loose ends, and he had heard no sound from the tobacco chewer.

Fifteen or twenty minutes passed, and then the door opened suddenly and the man who couldn't swim appeared. He peered out the door a moment before coming out on deck.

"John," he called thickly, "where th' fuck are ye?"

Winchester remained motionless.

"John?"

"He probably fell overboard," the woman called from within, and she laughed at the thought. "Went out to pee and fell in the river," she laughed again.

"Shit," the man at the door said. He came out of the cabin and closed the door, staggered to the boat railing and looked up and down the river. "John?" he called.

Winchester came up behind the man and gouged the bone handle of the knife into his lower back. "Jump in the river," he said.

The man stiffened and did not speak for a moment, then he said, "Oh, shit. Not again."

Winchester chuckled dryly, slipped his arm almost gently around the drunk's neck, and drew the blade

106

of the knife across his throat.

The man who couldn't swim died on his feet, spewed blood from his nose and mouth, and Winchester caught him by the belt and heaved him over the rail into the water.

He watched him drift down the river, leaving a trail of blood dissipating behind him.

"Guess you never will learn to swim," Winchester said, and turned back to the cabin door.

There was no sound from within now, none at all. Winchester's eyes searched the boat, the river all around it, and the nearby bank, but he saw nothing, no sound and no movement.

Where was the tobacco chewer?

He turned to the door and pushed it open, stepping out of line with the opening as he did so in case anyone should have a gun trained on the door.

"Virgil, is that you?" the woman asked.

Winchester did not show himself.

"Who's there?"

Carefully, he put an eye around the corner and peered into the dimly-lighted interior. The woman was sitting up on a cot in the corner, a dirty blanket pulled around her skinny body. Her legs were drawn up in front of her and her arms wrapped around her knees.

The cabin was sparsely furnished. There was nothing but a cookstove, a couple of cots, and a pile of dirty blankets in the corner. There was nowhere that a man could hide.

Winchester stepped into the cabin, knife in hand, and the woman's face went a shade whiter. She drew away from him against the wall, a slatternly woman in her mid-thirties with stringy, brown hair and a mouthful of rotten teeth.

She clutched the blanket to her chest with grimy hands. "It's you," she hissed.

"In the flesh," Winchester said lightly. "And you and I, I think we have a score to settle, don't we? Got an empty whiskey bottle around?"

"Please, mister, I didn't know who you were. I though you were a robber. We still got your guns— and your bedroll, too."

"Where's Hiram?"

"Hiram? Why—he left—early this morning."

He took a menacing step toward her, lifted the knife.

"Please, mister—I swear, I'm tellin' the truth. Hiram rode out early this morning. He didn't say where he was goin'—he just rode out. He was gone when I woke up."

She scrambled off the cot, clutching the blanket around her, and snatched up Winchester's bedroll where it lay against the wall. "Here—it's all here— everything—you can have everything."

"Everything?"

"Yes, everything. Look—" she dropped the blanket a little and revealed her knobby breasts—"I'll make it up to you—anything you want."

"Well," Winchester said seriously, "I might be persuaded to take a little of what you owe me out in trade. But there's just one thing."

"Anything . . . anything you want."

"You'll have to get your pussy wet for me."

She giggled. "Sure, mister. But you can help me a little with that, can't you?"

"You bet I can," he said, and reached for her.

"Hey, don't be so rough!"

He caught her by a skinny arm and jerked, then shoved her ahead of him out the cabin door. She lost her hold on the blanket she held around her, and he saw that she was naked underneath.

When she realized what he intended she began to struggle, planting her feet against the deck and bracing like a calf balking on a rope. "Let go of me, you bastard!" she screeched.

He manhandled her on toward the boat railing, and she screamed in terror and clawed at him with broken nails. He avoided her flailing arms, gripped the back of her neck with one hand and her naked ass with the other.

After a short struggle, he got the woman positioned on the top railing of the deck, planted a boot against her backside and kicked her, butt over teakettle, into the river.

There was a tremendous splash as she landed in the water, followed by a flurry of flailing arms and legs. She screeched obscenities at him, and he stood by the rail and smiled, waved an arm to her until she drifted out of hearing.

He went into the cabin then and caught up his rifle, and after some rummaging found his Colt .45 with the cutaway trigger guard. He shoved the gun into his empty holster and went back out on deck.

After tugging the keelboat near the bank, he leaped ashore, still keeping a sharp eye out. The tobacco chewer was apparently gone, probably to rejoin Scarface, but one never knew.

Almost as an afterthought, Winchester pulled the

knife from his boot and slashed the rope that held the keelboat to the bank. If anyone returned here there would be nothing left for them.

The dilapidated craft moved sluggishly out into the river and started downstream. After a few minutes the boat encountered the quicker current in the middle of the river and jerked with the impact. It was if a hand had grabbed it and pulled. The boat began moving perceptibly faster.

He went back to where he had left the gray, mounted up, and started back down the river. The tobacco chewer had eluded him again, but this time he had a good idea where he had gone, and Winchester had no intention of following.

He would play the game their way now. He would let Scarface come to him on his own terms, and he would be waiting.

If the dugout in the cutbank was warm by night, it was steamy by day. Julia at last wriggled completely free of the filthy blankets and sat up. Sweat was streaming down her face, and she could feel it trickling down her body inside the tattered blouse.

Moses and Pete were playing cards at the table, ignoring her. They rarely spoke to one another, and Julia had become so bored with her captivity that she felt she could absolutely die!

It had taken her a long time to accept the death of her mother at the hands of these men, but now that she had, she was having a harder time accepting her own situation. She had been pulled violently out of a civilized world consisting of well-mannered gentle-

110

men and giggling girlfriends and cast here in this place, bound hand and foot. She had been pawed, mauled, and generally treated in ways that she had never knew existed in her other world.

She knew that she looked a fright with her dirty hair falling any way it would. The dress she wore, which had once been fresh and pretty, was now filthy and in tatters, almost falling off her, there was so little of it left.

There was only one thing that she was thankful for. Since Hiram had departed she had not been ill-treated, but she had been watched closely. Moses did not trust her, for he knew that she was simply biding her time, waiting for another chance.

Just a single moment of inattention by them was all that she wanted, but there had been none. Her hands were loosened long enough for her to prepare the meals, eat, and clean up afterward, and she was watched every minute of that time. When she was finished she was immediately tied up.

Julia watched them as they sat at the table. Moses was dealing the cards nervously. She had noticed that he had been on edge the last couple of days. She believed that they were expecting Hiram, and he had not returned.

Also, Moses had not been the same since she had told him about James Winchester. She had come to believe that Moses was, indeed, the scarfaced man that the infamous Winchester searched for. Moses seemed to live in fear of the name Winchester, and he did not cover his feelings well. Her barbs had elicited tremendous anger from the man, and she had been afraid to taunt him further.

When she stopped to look at it logically, Julia realized that it actually remained only a dream of hers. Except for the fact that the scarfaced man was here, she had no hard evidence whatever that suggested her cousin Winchester might be on their trail. It was merely wishful thinking.

Suddenly, Julia was startled out of the wells of thought by hoofbeats outside the dugout. Her heart sank. She had wished all worlds of evil to befall the tobacco chewer while he was gone, but it seemed that all her wishful thinking ever accomplished was to occupy her mind.

Moses turned over his chair getting up. He jerked open the door and looked out. "Where in the everlastin' Jesus have you been?"

Hiram staggered in the door, looking drawn and pale. His right hand was wrapped in a bloody bandage, but there was a grin that split his face from ear to ear.

"It's a long story, Mose," he said, "but I think it's one you're gonna like."

"I'll be the judge of that," Moses snapped. "Get on with it. You're gonna be the death of me yet. Send you off on a simple, goddamned errand an' it takes you a week to get back an' you get shot up in the process! What the hell happened?"

"Just simmer down, now Mose! I'll tell you." Hiram sat down at the table and started to unfold his story.

When he reached the part where he had taken a shot at Winchester in Council Bluffs, Moses interrupted him. "*You what*?" he almost shouted. "Have you lost what feeble mind you've got left? You want to get us all killed?"

Hiram held up a hand. "Just wait a minute. I ain't through yet. He got on my trail, see, and I hid out at that boat on the river above Winony, you know the one — with the Morris brothers and their scalawag sister."

"And?"

"That's where I got this." He held up his bandaged hand. "Winchester tracked me there and got the drop on me, shot off one of my fingers. He would have shot off more, too, but that Doris, she laid for him with a whiskey bottle from behind, and after she knocked him in the river, I grabbed up his own rifle and blowed his brains out with it . . . killed' im, I did!"

Moses was not impressed. "How do you know you killed him? You thought you were going to kill him in Council Bluffs."

"I swear I did, Mose. I shot him in the head. I seen the blood fly, and it was a .44 Henry. No man could live after that."

Moses looked at the other man at the table. "What do you think, Pete?"

Pete shrugged. "Anything's possible. You believe what you want. Me, I won't count Jim Winchester dead unless I lay the coins on his eyelids, myself."

As Hiram relayed his story, Julia's hopes rose and fell. Winchester *had* been looking for them. It was almost too good to be true. But as Hiram kept talking, her joy was short-lived. If he had, in fact, killed Winchester, her last prayer was gone.

She drew back against the wall, shivering even though it was hot in the dugout. If her father did pay

113

the ransom, what would they do with her? Rape? Murder? She certainly expected no better than what they had given her mother. They had proven that they were capable of anything, and for that reason Julia had little hope for her survival.

Her last and only hope was escape. But how? She had had absolutely no opportunity since the last time she had tried, and she did not expect any.

Moses walked to the door of the dugout and looked contemplatively out at the sunbaked draw. Without turning around, he said, "You delivered the note to Strawbridge, like I said?"

Hiram nodded. "He'll find it. I slipped it under the front door and knocked."

"All right. Strawbridge will have the money at Winona tomorrow if he's going to pay."

"And he might have more than the money," Pete said suddenly. "He might have Winchester."

Hiram slapped his good hand on the table. "I tell you, Winchester's *dead*! I killed him myself."

Pete gave him a look that would have withered a corn crop.

"Pete, you and I will ride for Winona," Moses said. "Hiram can stay here and watch the girl until we come back with the money."

"Aw, Mose, how come I allus—"

"You shut up and do what I tell you! You've caused me enough worry the last couple of days. You watch that girl and watch her close. She's sneaky. But don't you do nothin' to her until we get back with the money."

"And what happens then?"

"After we get the cash you can have what you've

114

been a-hankerin' for all along, but not a minute sooner. You understand me?"

Hiram bobbed his head, grinned. "You bet. I've waited this long. I can wait a few more hours easy."

"See that you do."

Pete and Moses went out, and minutes later, Julia heard the tattoo of departing horses. Hiram stood in the doorway until they had passed out of hearing.

When they were gone, he turned around slowly and grinned at her. "Well now, it's just you an' me, honey. Like I told you before, ol' Mose can't always be around to take care of you."

"Didn't you hear what he said?" Julia said faintly. "You can't touch me until they get the money."

"Why, I don't recall Moses sayin' that. Iffin' he did it weren't what he meant, nosirree. What he meant was, I can't have it *all* until he gets the money. I don't recall him sayin' I couldn't *touch* you."

He started walking toward her, grinning, and a clammy hand gripped Julia's entrails. He knelt beside her and caught the cloth of her dress in his good hand and jerked, bared her to the waist.

He pulled her head into the crook of his arm and pressed the tobacco stench of his mouth to hers, his hand seeking the softness of her breast.

Chapter 11

It was almost noon the following day when Winchester returned to the ferry at Winona. The sun was hot, and heat waves shimmered on the river, danced like tiny devils.

After his swim in the river, the gash on Winchester's head had broken open and bled a little, and he had rebandaged it as best he could.

He unsaddled the gray behind Bartlett's cabin, rubbed him down, and turned him loose in the corral with Bartlett's mule. Also in the corral were two other mounts that had been recently ridden. They were still wet with lather.

When he walked around the cabin the first person he saw in the yard was Robert Strawbridge, talking with Bartlett.

Strawbridge looked at him. "What happened to you?"

"Had a little set-to with our friend the tobacco chewer and some friends of his."

"The same man who spit on the walls at the house?"

"The same. He was the man who delivered the ransom note to you."

"Did you kill him?"

Winchester shook his head. "No, he got away, but some of his friends weren't so lucky."

Strawbridge looked puzzled, but Winchester did not offer to explain further.

"I talked to a couple of men on a mackinaw this morning," Amos Bartlett said. "They was tellin' me about a sidewheeler that fished a woman out of the river about dawn this morning. Said she was buck-naked, nigh drowned, and madder than an ol' settin' hen. You wouldn't know anything about that, would you?"

Winchester grinned but shook his head in the negative. "What kind of low-life bastard would do a thing like that to a lady?"

"I never said anything about a lady." Bartlett winked.

Winchester turned back to Strawbridge. "Did you bring the money?"

"It's in the house. Twenty-thousand — all I could get together on such short notice. Most of my money is tied up in stock."

They went inside the cabin where Strawbridge opened a brown briefcase that was lying on the bed. It was lined with stacks of new currency, the most money Winchester had ever seen in one place before.

Bartlett whistled. "Chrissakes, but I'm a blessed man! Never thought I'd lay eyes on that much money."

"Bartlett," Winchester asked him, "have you got an old gallon jug, a liquor jug with a ring in the top?"

"Why, sure, somewhere around. What the dickens you want with that?"

He never had a chance to answer, for at that moment

118

there came a voice from the kitchen doorway behind him.

"Jim?"

The hair prickled on the back of his neck at the familiar ring, and he turned around slowly. After a moment he found his voice. "What the hell are you doing here?"

"Don't hold it against me," Strawbridge said. "It was all her idea, and nothing I said would change her mind. I learned a long time ago not to argue with a woman, and she said she was a friend of yours."

"Don't be angry, Jim," the woman continued. "Forgive me for being a busybody, but I picked the letter out of my stove and read what was left of it. I was afraid for you, and I want to help."

"Rosie, damnit —"

Rose McEachen closed the space between them and threw her arms around his neck, hugged him fiercely, cut his anger with her short.

She was wearing a fresh, new dress, and she felt wonderful pressed against him. The woman smell of her hair began to arouse him immediately, and he pushed her back.

"You've got no business out here, Rose. What do you want to do, get yourself killed?"

"Me? What about yourself? Look at you. You're an absolute fright, gone to skin and bone. How long has it been since you've ate?"

He shrugged. "I can take care of myself."

"I'll bet." She turned away, her golden curls flouncing haughtily. "You men carry on. I'm going to help Little Swallow fix something." She looked levelly at Winchester. "And you're going to eat and rest a little."

This time he didn't argue, and she disappeared back

119

into the kitchen. When she was gone, Amos Bartlett caught his eye and grinned.

Winchester felt himself flushing. "Fool woman," he muttered.

"You're a lucky man," Strawbridge said. "There's not many would traipse after a body like that. She took the boat from Fort Pierre to Council Bluffs, looked me up and demanded to know what the Sam Hill was going on. Nothing else would do her but to come with me here to meet you."

"She came at the right time," Winchester said grimly. "The chips are down now. They'll be here to collect tonight or early tomorrow. I'd guess tonight, under cover of darkness."

Amos Bartlett went out the door and returned a few minutes later with an empty whiskey jug of the kind the kidnappers had specified. It had a cork, and a ring in the top that a rope could be tied to.

"Damndest thing I ever heard of," Bartlett said.

"What do you figure they've got in mind, Jim?" Strawbridge asked.

"You've got me by the ass." Winchester started rolling the bills and stuffing them in the mouth of the jug. "I've never heard of anything like it, but whatever it is, I'm going to be waiting for them."

"You can bet your breeches they know that, too," Bartlett said. "They've got to have a way figured of getting that money and getting away with it."

That, Winchester reflected, was the twenty-thousand dollar question, and he was thus far completely exasperated by it. He had seen a lot of tricks over the last five years, but never anything that even remotely resembled this.

Scarface and the others knew that a trap would be set, they had to know. How did they plan on getting that jug of money out of the river and still avoid gunplay?

He had another thought. Maybe they had no intention of avoiding gunplay. Something about the entire setup worried him. Somewhere in the pantry he smelled a rat. Could it be *he* who was being set up for the kill? Was Scarface tired of being hounded and now bent on putting an end to it himself?

It was not something that Winchester had ever considered before. Was the scarfaced man now the hunter, and he the hunted? It was not impossible, for Scarface had proven himself canny in the past . . . very canny.

But if that be the case, Winchester would welcome the confrontation. It was what he had always wanted. Let the chips fall where they might. It would be this way in the end, anyway, just Scarface and himself, eye to eye, gun to gun. And when the smoke had cleared, it would be over, for better or worse. If Scarface died, it would be well, and if it were he who fell, it would still be just as over.

He had little fear of dying. He had always faced that possibility, and he did not care. He only knew that there must be an end to it, somehow, somewhere.

That evening, after the ransom was ready to go into the river and everyone had eaten, Winchester went out to the corral to tend his horse.

Rose McEachen followed him and leaned on the fence. "Jim, I want you to understand why I came. You believe it is the scarfaced man who is coming for that money, don't you?"

"I hope."

She nodded. "I hope it is, too, Jim. Believe that or not,

I want it for you. I know that there will be no hope for us until you have found him, and I just wanted to be here for your final triumph, or . . ."

"Or what?"

"Or your final defeat." She looked at the ground. "That is possible. You know that, don't you? You're only a man."

He nodded, busy rubbing down the gray. "I know I'm only a man, but I also know that Scarface is something less than a man."

"He haunts you, doesn't he?"

"Every day of my life, and most of the nights."

"How did you come to know that he was responsible for the death of your parents?"

He looked at her.

"Strawbridge," she explained, "he told me everything. If you had done that three years ago it would have saved me a lot of sleepless nights. I would have understood you better."

"It wasn't your problem, and it still isn't. It's no one's but my own."

"There you go, cutting me out again."

He stood up and took a deep breath, looked off across the river for a moment, then walked over to the fence. "All right, it was like this. A couple of days before my parents were killed Scarface came to our house. He was somehow connected with my father's business. They argued about something—I can't remember what. I was too young for the argument to mean anything to me, but I heard the scarfaced man threaten my father. But Pa didn't scare easy . . . he told Scarface to go straight to hell."

"And?"

122

"Two days later he was dead. He and Mother boarded the steamboat *Golden Boy* for her maiden journey up-river. They had no sooner cleared the dock than she blew. Somebody planted enough explosives in the hull of that boat to blow up an entire town."

Rose looked skeptical. "How do you know it was your parents who were meant to be killed that day? It could have been someone else, and they just two of the many innocent victims. There were other innocent victims aboard, weren't they?"

He nodded. "Yes, there were others, but I saw something else, too. I saw Scarface after the boat was blown up. I saw him leaning against the side of a warehouse, laughing. There was no one around him that he could have been talking with. He was just standing there laughing to himself like it was all a big joke, not five minutes after the explosion. I know it was him."

"That kind of evidence wouldn't hold water in court, Jim Winchester," she said, matter-of factly. "It's circumstantial, all of it."

"True," he said, "but sometimes that's all you need. I know what I know. Besides, it's never going to court. I don't have that to worry about."

"So you're going to be judge, jury, and executioner."

He pointed a finger at her. "Right. The law had their turn, and they came up empty. No suspects, no arrests. Now it's my turn."

He watched her walk back to the cabin dejectedly. He had never told anyone as much as he had just told her, and probably for the reasons she had just pointed out. To anyone else, all his evidence looked like mere speculation and conjecture, but not to him. He knew what he knew. More than just the evidence itself, and the dreams that haunted him, he *knew* it. He felt it in his bones. If it were not true, why had Scarface evaded him for five years? If he were innocent, Winchester was sure the man would have confronted him at some time and denied the charges.

When he finished tending his horse, he found a twenty-foot length of rope and carried it back to the cabin. He made sure the whiskey jug full of money was corked tightly, and then he tied the end of the rope in the jug handle.

Strawbridge watched him. "What now?" he asked.

"We wait for the night," Winchester said. "I have no idea how they are planning to get this money, but I'll bet my last dollar they make their play in the dark. That's the kind of men they are."

Rose McEachen made no further attempt to talk to him. She helped the Indian girl, Little Swallow, in the kitchen, and stayed out of his way.

Winchester cleaned his rifle and handgun and loaded them both while he waited. Robert Strawbridge carried a rifle, and he did the same.

Amos Bartlett took down his ancient, Greener shotgun from the antler rack on the cabin wall. He broke open the action and peered down the twin barrels.

"Bartlett," Winchester said, "this is no fight of yours. You've done enough, letting us stay here. We don't expect any help when it comes to gunplay."

"Boy," the whiskered old man replied, "that wasn't the way it was done in my day. If a man came to your house an' he had troubles, they became your troubles if you took him in. When folks come a-gunnin' for visitors under my roof, that just naturally makes me mad. They're a-goin' to have me to lick, too."

124

Winchester said no more. If the man had made up his mind there was no sense arguing.

At sunset, he took up the jug of money and his rifle and went down to the river. He tied the rope to a piling underneath the ferry dock and dropped the jug into the river with care.

The whiskey jug sank momentarily, then bobbed back up and floated downstream. It reached the end of the rope and stopped, bobbed side to side with the pull of the current. The rope was pulled partially taut.

"Well," Robert Strawbridge said, behind him, "there it is, you bastards. Come and get it." The little, bald man was suddenly angry. The knuckles of his pudgy hands turned white where they gripped the rifle.

"Might as well find a good spot and settle in for the night," Winchester said. "Find a place where that jug will never leave your sight, not even for a minute. Lord knows what they've got in mind."

Winchester went about twenty-five yards upstream of the dock and settled his back against the trunk of a willow that overhung the river. He did not intend to get far away from that money. From his position, he could see the jug bobbing underneath the dock, and Robert Strawbridge on the other side of it, nestled behind a thick stand of cattail. Old Amos Bartlett had taken up a position closer to the cabin but within sight of the dock.

Darkness fell rapidly, closed like a great, black hand over the river. The sun sank from sight, left only a heavy, red glow in the west momentarily, and then it, too, was gone.

The chill that surrounded the river settled over Winchester's shoulders like a wet blanket, and soon he was holding his hands between his thighs to warm them, shivering with the cold. He had neglected to bring a jacket or blanket.

About midnight, Rose McEachen brought him some coffee, and he accepted the hot cup gratefully. Over her other arm she carried an old buffalo robe, and he took that, too.

"It's quiet," she said.

"Yeah," he answered, sipping the coffee. The hot liquid burned his lips, but he liked the feel of it going down his throat and warming his insides.

"When do you think they'll come?"

"Your guess is as good as mine."

"Jim?"

He looked up at her, and she knelt quickly and kissed him on the mouth. "Be careful," she said, and then she turned and went back to the cabin.

Winchester finished his coffee, and for about the tenth time checked the action of his rifle by moonlight.

About an hour after Rose left, he heard another step on the riverbank and looked around. It was the Indian girl, Little Swallow, and she stopped about twenty feet from where he sat and just stood there a moment, looking at him. He could not make out the expression on her face, but he could feel the haunting question in her dark eyes.

At last, she spoke, in halting English. "Rose . . . Rose—she is—your woman?"

He thought for a moment, then nodded. "My woman."

The Indian looked at him another long moment, then turned and walked quietly away.

Now what the hell had all that been about? Winchester shrugged and went back to watching the jug. Women seemed to think that when they slept with a man, he owed them something. Hell, he had not asked the little squaw to come to his bed. She had come for a reason, got what she wanted, and left. That was all there was to it as far as he was concerned.

He had to admit, though, the girl was pretty in a bizarre sort of way, but Rose was here now . . . and that was the end of that. When Rose had shown up it had upset his and Little Swallow's playhouse, so to speak.

As the hours passed, Winchester found himself getting drowsy. He dozed for a few minutes once and panicked when he awoke. But when he looked out underneath the dock, the jug was still there, bobbing in the water.

In the cold, gray hours before dawn he tried to keep his eyes open but could not. The long hours without rest or food had taken their toll, as well as the head injury he had sustained.

He slept soundly, for how long he did not know, and it was a gunshot that woke him . . . a shot from across the river.

He came to his feet, still half asleep, and grabbed for his rifle. Dawn had broken in the east, and it was already almost fully light.

He cast a glance toward the dock and saw that the jug was still where he had left it.

Another rifle report broke the stillness. The marksman was on the other side of the river, but Winchester could not tell what he was shooting at.

At him? No bullets had even come close. He looked toward the cabin. There was no one in sight.

Suddenly, Strawbridge stood up from his position behind the cattails and called, "Jim?"

Winchester looked at him.

"Jim, they're shooting the damn rope in two!"

The rifle cracked again, but he still could not locate the marksman's position. He looked at the rope and saw that it was frayed badly at a point halfway between the piling and the jug.

He broke into a run for the dock, and just as he reached it, a heavy-caliber bullet showered him with splinters, and he took a headlong dive into the river.

He heard the rifle bark again as he swam for the piling where the rope was tied. He reached out for the rope as the rifle spoke again . . . caught it . . . and it went slack in his hand.

The last bullet had cut the rope in half, and the jug floated free, moved slowly out into the current and started downstream.

Winchester turned and made the riverbank again as another bullet showered him with water and mud. He scrambled up on the bank and broke into a run downstream, staying near the water's edge, trying to keep the whiskey jug in sight.

He had dropped his rifle somewhere, and his hand sought the gun at his side, breathed a sigh of relief when he found it still in the holster.

It had been a good trick. Their intentions were clear to him now. One man had shot the rope in half, and another, or perhaps more than one, would be waiting downstream, probably in a boat . . . waiting for twenty-thousand dollars to float into their hands.

Chapter 12

A mile below the ferry, the jug floated near the bank among some reeds. It dipped and swirled between the rocks where the water was only two or three feet deep.

Still in a dead run and gasping for breath, Winchester splashed into the shallow area of the river. He had lost his hat, and there was searing pain in his lungs as he tried to regain his breath. He had already wished a dozen times that he had caught his horse. In the suddenness of the moment he had not been thinking straight.

The whiskey jug dipped around some slippery rocks just out of his reach, and Winchester slipped and fell, splashed water like a tree falling and got himself thoroughly wet.

He scrambled after the jug again and this time caught the length of rope that trailed from the handle. He pulled the jug to him and stood up in the knee-deep water, dripping and shivering with the cold.

Suddenly, loud on the bank behind him, he heard the unmistakable click of a hammer being drawn back.

"Well, well," a voice said, "if it ain't Jim Winchester. Fella told me you was dead."

Winchester turned around slowly and saw a harmless-looking little man sitting a big appaloosa. He was dressed in old brogans, faded overalls, and a slouch hat. The only thing noticeable about him was his eyes, hard little gimlets of gray, and the rifle that he covered Winchester so casually with.

Winchester's guts twisted in a hard knot, and he stared at the man in disbelief. "Hello, Earl," he said at last. "You're a long way from home, aren't you?"

The man grinned. "Things got a little hot for me down in Arizona. You know how it is. They hire a man's gun, but when the job's done they don't want you around anymore."

"I know." Winchester looked across the river, then at the end of the frayed rope dangling in the water. "I might've known it was you. I never knew of many who could shoot a rifle like that."

The man chuckled. "Fell for it hook, line, and sinker, didn't you?"

"What do you mean?"

He chuckled again. "Ain't you a sight now, standin' there dripping like a wet dog . . . and holdin' an empty whiskey jug in your hand."

"It's not empty. We were out to keep our end of the bargain, if you were out to keep yours."

"Better look again, friend."

Winchester frowned, puzzled, but he took hold of

the cork in the jug's mouth and pulled it out. He peered inside.

Empty. Bone dry and empty as a tomb.

He cursed. "What the—"

"You'll understand, soon enough. Meantime—" the man's voice turned dangerous— "stay off my trail, Jim. I don't cotton to being followed. You and I were friends once. Let's keep it that way. I don't want to have to kill you."

"Nor I, you. But you haven't given me much choice, Earl. Why did you have to start murdering women. I thought you were a better man than that."

"I had nothing to do with that. The killing was all Moses' and Hiram's doing. I was only in it for the ransom of the girl. Times are hard, Jim, but I never meant to be a part of any rape and murder. I just fell in with some bad company. I've got no use for 'em, but I need the money."

"That doesn't make it look any better on you. Men have been hung for less."

"Not me, Jim. I'm not the hanging kind. Somebody may kill me, but I'll never swing."

"Which one of your partners chews tobacco?" Winchester asked.

"Hiram, why?"

"Then Moses is the man with the scar on his face?"

"Looks like you've been doing your homework."

"What's his last name?"

The man thought for a moment. "Gann, I believe it is. I've only heard it a couple of times." He looked at Winchester. "You think he's the one you've been huntin' all these years?"

"I was hoping you could tell me that."

131

Earl shook his head. "I've only known him a couple of months. Don't know anything about his past."

Winchester started to walk out of the river, but the little man hefted his rifle. "Stay where you are 'til I'm gone."

He stopped. He knew better than to take Earl Langley's words lightly.

"Take out your pistol with two fingers and throw it up here."

He considered going for it, but after a moment decided against it. With anyone else, maybe, but not with this man. He took the gun out carefully and tossed it up on the riverbank.

"Now," Earl said, "I'm here to tell you where you can find the girl." He did so briefly, then said, "Hiram, the one who chews tobacco, will be there at the dugout with her, but I don't expect he'll give you any trouble. He just needs a good, light killin'."

The man started backing the appaloosa away from the riverbank. "Remember what I said, Winchester. I don't want to look back and see you behind me. I don't want to kill you, but I don't take kindly to being hunted." He turned his horse around, but the rifle remained trained on Winchester's brisket, unwavering. "By the way, the next time you see me, the name's Pete." With that, he laid his heels to the appaloosa and lit out down the river.

Winchester made no attempt to pursue. He climbed out of the water, picked up his gun, and shoved it back into the holster. He looked at the empty whiskey jug in his hand, then threw it disgustedly at the rocks. It shattered, and the pieces floated out into the river.

He started walking back toward the ferry.

Earl Langley.

That was just who he didn't need in his way right now. He had known Langley in the sheep and cattle wars down in New Mexico and Arizona. The man was an old he-coon from the high country, and probably the best damned hand with any kind of a shooting iron that he had ever seen.

Langley was fast with a six-gun, maybe faster than he was, but he did not want to think about that. Scarface was out there somewhere, and neither Earl Langley nor the devil himself was going to stand in his way.

Halfway back to the ferry, he met Rose McEachen running toward him. She was pale and out of breath. He caught her by the shoulders and waited until she could speak.

"It's Bartlett," she gasped finally. "After the shooting started, he chased all the horses out of the corral and stampeded them. When Strawbridge ran up to ask what he was doing, Bartlett clubbed him in the head with his gun butt. Then him and Little Swallow took off."

"Which way did they go?"

She pointed southwest, into Nebraska. "What's going on, Jim?"

Bartlett! So that had been their game. Langley had said he would understand soon enough.

He explained to her on the way back to the ferry. "They've got the money, Bartlett and Little Swallow. He must have switched jugs on me somehow before I put it in the river."

133

"The Bartletts were in on it all the time, then?"

"Looks that way." He told her of the empty whiskey jug, and his meeting with Earl Langley.

"Langley is one of them? He's a dangerous man, isn't he? I've heard of him."

Winchester nodded. "In a showdown, they don't come any worse than Langley. I saw him gun down two men and wound a third in a shootout in Arizona, and those three weren't tinhorns, either."

Back at the cabin, they found Robert Strawbridge semi-conscious and nursing an ugly gash on his forehead. The cut was bleeding profusely, and he was trying to staunch the flow with a kerchief.

He looked up as they approached. "We've been played for a pack of fools, Winchester," he said, accusingly.

Winchester nodded. "It was a good trick, all right."

"That goddamn Bartlett was convincing, wasn't he?" Rose McEachen said.

"That's another hide I'm going to nail to the barn door."

Robert Strawbridge snorted to himself.

"Just one good thing came of this," Winchester went on. "I know where your daughter is. As soon as I catch my horse, I'm going to get her."

Strawbridge came to his feet but had to catch on to a porch post to keep from falling. "I'm going with you, then. More and more of late I've come to doubt your capabilities, Winchester. I believe that you're more legend than you are truth."

Winchester looked at him coldly. "You're in no shape to ride anywhere, and I don't want you holding me up. I want you to catch the next boat back to

Council Bluffs and wait there for your daughter. Rose will go with me, and she'll bring Julia back to you."

"Where are you going?"

"Didn't you offer me twenty-thousand to bring Julia back alive?"

Strawbridge nodded.

"And didn't you say that twenty-thousand in ransom was all you could raise?"

Another nod.

He grinned humorlessly. "Then the way I figure it, those folks have twenty-thousand dollars that belong to me, and I aim to have it."

"Don't let him kid you," Rose told Strawbridge. "It's got nothing to do with the money. He'd be going after Scarface if he had to *pay* twenty-thousand."

Abruptly, Winchester turned away from them and went to the corral where he picked up the tracks of the horses. He recognized the hoofprints of the gray easily and followed them to the rocky hill behind the cabin. The gelding, he knew, would not have gone far. That horse would discover quickly that something was amiss and turn around and come back. He would not stray far from the hand that fed him.

At the top of the hill, Winchester gave a shrill whistle and waited, but there was no immediate response. He followed the tracks a quarter-mile farther and whistled again.

This time, he heard the drum of hoofbeats not far off, and the gray gelding came to him on the run. He slipped the hackamore he had brought along over the horse's head and mounted him bareback.

He rode back toward the corral and picked up the tracks of another horse. Fifteen minutes later and not

135

a mile away, he found the animal in a coulee not far from the river. It was Rose McEachen's bay mare.

Returning to the cabin, he scanned the ground for more tracks, but all that remained was the trail of two horses headed southwest, side by side. Bartlett had stolen the mount that had belonged to Strawbridge, evidently for Little Swallow to ride.

Winchester saddled the two remaining horses and led them back to the cabin where Rose waited for him. They mounted up, and he lifted a hand to Strawbridge. "Don't worry about the twenty-thousand you owe me. Like I said, I'll collect it from Scarface."

"And if you don't?"

He shrugged. "If I don't, you won't have to worry. I won't be alive to spend it."

They rode out due northwest with the sun hot on their backs. It was midday, and according to Earl Langley, they had forty miles to cover before nightfall.

Rose McEachen rode straight in the saddle beside him, her yellow curls bouncing with the gait of her horse, and for once, Winchester was glad of the company. He had been a long time alone, but this girl beside him was the closest bond he had with humanity.

He wondered suddenly, as she had, what did lie ahead for him. Would he kill the Scarface and ride free of the dreams that haunted him? Or would it be he who fell, killed by Scarface or Earl Langley?

He had never been a man to doubt his own capabilities, but the possibility was always there. He was, as Rose had pointed out, only a man.

Was he as good with a gun as Earl Langley? Somehow, Winchester did not believe he was as fast, but speed was many times not the decisive factor in a gunfight. A man had to be accurate as well, and sometimes it depended on how tough or determined he was. Simply, how much lead he could take without dying.

After an hour of hard riding, they slowed their horses to a walk to give them a breather.

After a moment, Rose McEachen spoke. "Jim, I've got something to tell you."

He waited.

"On the way to Winona, Robert Strawbridge and I did a lot of talking about you. Your uncle had something that he desperately wanted to tell you, but he was afraid to."

"Afraid?"

"He was afraid that you would kill him."

Winchester frowned. "What the hell could he tell me that would make me want to kill him?"

"It's a long story, Jim, and he told me all of it. He asked me to tell you when the opportunity was right, and let the chips fall where they may. You may still want to kill him after you hear, but I hope I can persuade you not to."

"Would you get on with it, for Chrissake!"

"You are a rich man, James Winchester."

"What are you talking about?"

She took a deep breath and began, going all the way back to the beginning, when he had lived with the Strawbridges after the death of his parents. She told him how Amanda Strawbridge had pressured Robert into using the money that rightfully belonged to their nephew, Robert's own feelings about it, and ended with, "And now that Amanda is dead, he wants to make it right. He wants to give you what is yours."

Winchester was silent for a long minute, stunned. Finally, all he could say was, "Well, I'll be god-damned."

"You can see why he was afraid to tell you," Rose went on. "It's enough to make a preacher mad. I'll have to admit, I did a bit of swearing at him myself, when he told me. I know something of the kind of life you've led the past few years, and how it could have all been different, but for him."

Winchester's face worked. "I would probably have gunned him down."

"I thought you might, but there's no point in it, Jim—no point at all. Robert Strawbridge is a weak, spineless man who operated under pressure from his wife. His own conscience has suffered for years, but Amanda was his strength. She would not allow him to break. If you're going to hate either of them, hate Amanda."

He took a deep breath. "I've spent over five years starving, freezing, part of the time with not a red cent in my pocket. And now I find out that all the time I was a rich man."

Rose was silent for a long time as they continued to walk their horses, leaving him alone with his thoughts. But unknown to her, Winchester was not thinking at all. He was numb inside, still not sure what had hit him, or what to do about it. It was the damndest feeling he had ever experienced.

At last, she said, "What will you do, Jim?"

"I don't know . . . I just don't know."

"Don't kill Strawbridge, Jim, please. It would serve no purpose."

After a moment, he shook his head angrily. "I don't have time to think about it now. First comes Scarface and Earl Langley."

Rose McEachen turned a tear-streaked face to him and almost screamed the words. "But Jim, there's no need! Don't you understand? You're *rich*! Why must you continue with this senseless manhunt?"

"How much money I have makes no difference, Rosie. There's still Scarface . . . and there always will be until he's dead."

Winchester laid his heels to the gray gelding's sides, and the startled horse leaped into a run, leaving Rose McEachen behind. It angered him suddenly to admit it, but he must be developing a soft spot for women. Here he was, running off to save a girl who had probably already been molested, if not worse, while Scarface was getting farther away from him with every minute that passed.

All because of a snip of a girl . . . a girl who meant nothing to him, someone he did not even know. On top of that, the daughter of the man who, he had just learned, had practically stolen his life from him.

Damn!

Well, Scarface had waited for over five years. He supposed he could wait a little longer.

Chapter 13

Dust motes danced in the swath of sunlight that fell through the open door of the dugout, and Julia Strawbridge stared at them as if in a trance. How long it had been since Hiram's last attack she did not remember, nor did she wonder how long it would be until the next one. She had lost all will and all caring; she had ceased to struggle, for it was useless.

The man had not raped her . . . yet. He was wary of Moses, and he was simply waiting for the time that he could have what he wanted of her with Moses' blessing. But he had so assaulted her dignity in every other way that she felt she could be hurt little more by rape itself.

Sometimes she almost wished he would go ahead with it, if it would mean he would leave her alone afterward. But she was afraid that when he was finished he would kill her, as he had her mother.

She had reached the point where she would do practically anything if her captor would set her free in return, but she knew better than to try to make any deals with Hiram. He could not be trusted; it was useless to try.

She raised a hand to her battered face. It was bruised and swollen about the mouth, and when she touched her tongue to her lips she tasted blood mingled with Hiram's tobacco.

She was naked from the waist up, and little remained of the skirt that covered her legs. Her face and upper body were dirty and smudged with tobacco spittle from Hiram's mouth, the nipples of her breasts red and angry from pinches and bites. A trickle of blood was caked underneath the left one where the nipple had bled a little.

Moses and Pete had been gone since yesterday, and she prayed every minute for their return and an end to this horror. She would rather be dead than go on living like this. From the way the sun fell through the open door, it was now midafternoon.

She had slept little since the departure of Moses and Pete. Hiram had kept her up most of the preceding night. Because of Moses' warning, he had not performed the final violation of her, but he had an extremely dirty mind, and he had found other ways to amuse himself. He had forced her to perform an ungodly act on him with her mouth, the most disgusting and horrifying thing Julia had ever experienced, and afterward she had been violently sick.

He had laughed at her, and she had hated him with every fiber of her soul. Before Hiram, she did not know that she possessed the capability for such hate. The feelings that she held for him were indescribable; she had never despised another human being to the extent that she did him.

She was startled suddenly from her trance by a shadow that obliterated the ray of sunlight across the floor, and she closed her eyes and said another silent prayer.

Hiram came into the room. He had a worried look on his face, but his pig's eyes brightened when they fell on Julia in the corner where she had crawled with foolish hopes that he would not see her there.

"There you are, my little peach! Are you ready to play with your man, Hiram, again?" He came and knelt beside her and began to stroke her inner thigh. "I know you're hot for ol' Hiram, honey, but you'll just have to wait 'til Moses gits back, then I'll give you just what you ache for." He grinned, enjoying his little game. "It's hard on you, I know. Hell, me, too. But it'll happen soon, and it'll be worth waiting for, I guaran-tee. Anticipation, that's what makes it better."

Julia opened her eyes at last and looked at him. Her voice, when she spoke, was scarcely more than a whisper. "You still don't know, do you?"

"Know what?"

"How far did they have to go to get the money?"

"Forty miles, or thereabouts."

"It was noon yesterday when they left, Hiram, and now it's past noon today. How long do you figure it takes to ride forty miles?"

He frowned, getting her drift finally. "Now, you shet up that kind of talk. They'll be along soon enough, you'll see."

"They're not coming back, Hiram. You've been double-crossed. They're cutting you out. You know it, but you just don't want to believe it."

143

He slapped her, and her head rocked with the blow, but she felt no pain. The blows she received now only fell unnoticed by her numb body. Her brain was so dulled by endless pain that it was merely a part of her existence.

"They're not coming back for you, Hiram," she said again.

"Shut up!" He slapped her again. "I know what you're a-tryin' to do. You just want to turn us agin one another—cause bad blood between us. Well, it won't work, so hush!"

"Think about it, Hiram. Look how they've always treated you. Nothing you do suits Moses, and they never believe anything you say. Did they believe you when you told them you had killed Winchester?"

He shook his head. "No, but I damn sure did—kilt him with his own rifle."

"Sure, you did, Hiram. But did they believe you? No, they think Hiram is a fool, a little kid. They don't think you could do a job like that."

"Well, they'll believe me when they find out for themselves."

"Will they, Hiram? Then, they'll probably say it was someone else who killed Winchester, not you. They don't think you're a man. Look at where you are now. They left you here to watch me just to get you out of their way. They didn't want you along with them, Hiram. They don't like your company."

"That ain't so!"

"It is so, Hiram. You know it is. Why do you want to hang around men like that? You are a good, honest man. You deserve better friends than that, don't you?"

Hiram stared at her for a long minute, blinking his piggish eyes. She knew she had planted the seed of doubt in his feeble mind, whether he admitted it or not. Now she only had to let the seed mature.

He did not slap her again, but got up and went to the door, looked out of the wash to the north. After a moment he turned around. "It ain't so," he said, but his words were lifeless, without conviction. "I know what you're up to, an' you ain't a-foolin' ol' Hiram. Moses and Pete'll be along directly, and when they do I'm gonna make you wisht you had'na said all that."

He went back to the door and looked out again, his brow furrowed in thought. After a little, he went back outside without another word to her.

Julia was sure of nothing she had said, but she did have a nagging dread that the others would not return here after they collected the ransom. She had been gambling when she had sown the seeds of suspicion in Hiram's mind, for there was no predicting how he would react. He was mentally unbalanced, and no one knew that better than she.

Could she persuade him to release her if the others did not return, or would he simply kill her as he had Amanda? The possibility was there, if she played her cards right, but inevitably, he would rape her first. That, she realized, was unavoidable, for it was the single thing that he wanted most from her.

If she bestowed on him willingly the favor of her body, would he be grateful enough to release her? Her mind shrank from the idea; it smacked of compromise and the breaking of her spirit. But this was not civilization, it was barbarism, the survival of the strong and the crafty. And if she wanted to live,

145

she only had one commodity to bargain with . . . sex.

It was something Hiram wanted that only she could supply, and if he wanted it badly enough he would be willing to pay. But, of course, there was always the danger of the doublecross after he had had his way with her. She must think of something to prevent that.

But what?

As her mind struggled for an idea, afternoon waned into evening, and as the sun sank fiery red in the west, darkness began to gather around the door of the dugout.

Julia listened hopefully for the sounds of approaching horses, but she heard nothing, only the incessant rattle of the cicadas on the sod roof over her head.

Hiram returned to the dugout, stopped in the doorway and stared at her. "They ain't a-comin'," he said at last. "You was right. They ain't a-comin' back for us."

She nodded. "What will you do, Hiram?"

"I dunno." He closed the heavy door behind him.

"They've already collected the ransom by now. If you want your share of it you'll have to find them."

"And what'll I do with you, leave you here?"

"Free me, Hiram. That was the deal, wasn't it? When the ransom was collected, I was to be turned loose?"

"Yeah, but somethin' ain't right about that." He looked at her wickedly. "They've got the money, see, and I've got none of it. So I've come out in the hole, except for one thing."

"What's that?"

"I've got you. If I turned you loose I wouldn't have a goddamn thing to show for all this trouble, would I, no woman and no money either."

Julia's hopes fell. He was some brighter than she had credited him. It looked as if she would be forced to bargain with her hole card, the only thing she had left.

She at last accepted the fact that she had only her own resources to depend on. As in the books she had read, no knight in shining armor was coming to her rescue. Moses and Pete had given Hiram the double-cross. Moses would not be returning to save her from Hiram's advances. James Winchester, if he had ever been in the picture, was now dead, according to Hiram.

"Look," she said, in one last desperate attempt, "don't dig your grave deeper. I'll do anything you want in exchange for my life. You're already a wanted man, but if you kill me you won't even get a trial. You'll swing from the nearest tree. You know the laws of Nebraska where women are concerned."

He leered at her. "You think that makes any difference to me? I'll swing anyway, they ever catch me. I fucked and kilt your mother, don't you remember?"

"I remember, Hiram. But why kill me? I can't do you any harm. Without a horse, you could be two states away by the time I could walk for help."

"But there's always a chance I might not be two states away — a chance that's easy to eliminate."

A knot of fear balled itself in Julia's stomach. Would her end come just as her mother's, then? She had been sure she could bargain for her life, regard-

147

less of the cost. But her life, it seemed, was all that she could gain. Freedom was another matter. In that direction the only answer was escape. But she must have time for that . . . that was it, she must bargain for time.

With her swollen lips, Julia made her best effort at a smile. "Hiram," she said, "you know, if you let me live, we could have some times together, you and I. I'll go along with you — I'll go with you to find Moses and the others. You can be a man, Hiram. You can stick up for your share of that money, and then we can go away together. How much money have you got coming, Hiram?"

His brow furrowed as he figured for a moment. "Seven thousand," he said at last, "or thereabouts. Seven thousand dollars."

"Just think where we could go on seven thousand dollars. Why, we could go to Kansas City, and you could cut a swath no man would laugh at."

He grinned hugely. "I figured you would come around, by 'n by. But I know there's more to it that you ain't sayin', too. It's that money you got your eye on. I never knew a woman who wouldn't stop and take notice of a man with money, but that's all right, I reckon. Money talks when nothin' else will."

Julia considered and decided to play honest. "Why, of course, that's part of it, Hiram. I'd be a liar if I said it wasn't. But that's not all of it, either. You're a fine figure of a man, a man I'd be proud to walk beside in Kansas City. All I ask is that you don't hit me so much. I'll give you what you want. As a matter of fact, I've been hard-put to hold out on you these past couple of days, but a girl has to hold on to her

148

dignity, doesn't she?"

"Why, sure," he grinned. "You can keep your dignity, all I want is the pussy." He started to unbutton his shirt, slipped the filthy suspenders off his shoulders. "And since Moses ain't a-comin' back, I figure right now would be a just-right place to start."

He started for her, and the knot of bile in Julia's stomach squeezed tighter. She prayed for the strength to play the game out, prayed that she would not be sick and give herself away. She must not think about what was happening to her. She must take her mind to a far, faraway place, a place or a time when she had been happy.

She had never given herself to any man. Could she not use her imagination and pretend that this was the lover she wanted, the man she had waited all her life for?

If she could, she would be able to do it. It was only a matter of controlling her own mind. She would be a little girl again. She would play-act . . . that was it . . . pretend that she was somewhere else in a soft bed with . . . with . . .

Hiram dropped his pants and gunbelt to the floor. He reached for the waist of her skirt and jerked, and she lay naked and vulnerable on the hard-packed earth, her long-kept secret exposed at last.

She closed her eyes tight and tried to squeeze out reality. There was a great emptiness inside her, she told herself, an emptiness that needed to be filled.

Hiram's hands fell on her knees, and she let them go slack and be pulled apart. He lowered his bulk on top of her, and she reached out her arms and held him.

She felt something punching at her privates, and as reality tried to return, tears squeezed themselves out from under her eyelids.

There was a noise somewhere far away, and she opened her eyes suddenly. It was the sound of the door opening that she had heard . . . only a slight creak.

A man was standing there, just inside the door. Hiram had not heard him; he was still trying clumsily to gain entrance to her body.

Julia stared at the stranger, not knowing if she should believe what she was seeing. He was a tall man, spare in the hips but wide at the shoulder, with a flat, expressionless face and black eyes that chilled her to look into them.

The man drew his gun and spoke. "Oh, tobacco-man."

Hiram stiffened on top of her. "Moses?" he grunted. "I thought—" He scrambled off Julia, looked around. His eyes widened at what he saw, and he dove for his gunbelt on the floor.

Julia looked on in horror as the stranger fired, his expressionless visage never flinching.

Hiram never reached his gun. The bullet almost took his hand off. Hitting him in the wrist, the bone was snapped, and a spray of blood, bone, and ligament was carried to the wall behind him.

Hiram rolled naked against the wall, gripping his mangled arm, his face gone white. He stared at the stranger, and his mouth worked, but there was no voice to accompany it.

The stranger raised his gun again, wordlessly, and sighted coldly over the barrel.

Julia's scream was lost in the roar of the shot. Blood sprayed the side of her face, and tiny fragments of a soggy matter splattered on her arm.

She twisted her head, but only caught a fleeting glimpse of the carnage that had been Hiram's head before she fainted.

While Rose McEachen waited, Winchester caught the corpse by the feet and dragged it outside. The fat body of the tobacco chewer was splotched and grotesque in the fading light, not a pretty sight with the top of the head blown away and blood spattered over the entire upper body.

Winchester tied a short length of rope to one of the man's ankles, and the other end to his saddle. He mounted his horse and dragged the body away down the wash, only far enough to be out of sight of the women, and left it there for the buzzards.

When he returned to the dugout, Rose had covered the girl with a blanket and was washing her face with a cloth wet from his canteen.

He opened the door of the dugout wide so that the stench of gunsmoke and death could clear.

Rose looked up. "What did you do with him?"

"Left him down the draw a piece. A man like him don't deserve burying. I scarcely expect it, myself."

The girl regained consciousness slowly, and when she opened her eyes they held only the blank stare of idiocy. They were, Winchester thought, the eyes of a person almost insane.

She looked at him and screamed, then again . . . and a third time, the screams of an animal in pain.

At last Rose got her eyes off him and quieted her.

She began to babble. "You'll tell them, won't you?" she said, gripping the front of Rose's shirt. "You'll tell them he didn't make it? He never raped me . . . he tried but he didn't make it . . . he never, I swear . . . he —"

"I'll tell them," Rose said, "I promise, I'll tell everyone. He didn't do it."

The girl relaxed then, and within a few minutes fell into a deep sleep of utter exhaustion.

Rose McEachen looked up at him, her eyes big and caring. "Do you think we made it in time?"

Winchester shrugged uncomfortably. "I don't know. Maybe she'll remember more of what really happened later."

Rose looked back down at the head in her lap, pushed a strand of hair out of the filthy, but now peaceful, face.

"You'll have to take her back to Strawbridge, Rose. I've got to go on."

She nodded, not looking up. "I won't argue with you anymore, Jim. All I ask is that you come back to me, if you can."

Outside the dugout, the gray gelding nickered for him, and he started for the door, stopped and started to say something, then changed his mind and kept walking. She should understand by now.

There was no other way.

He mounted the gelding and turned him southeast into the moonless night. The demon that he knew as Scarface had had his last laugh.

Chapter 14

The party of four did little riding by day. They moved chiefly under cover of darkness, avoiding the occasional soddies that dotted the Nebraska plains, except now and then to steal a few "roasting ears" from a sodbuster's corn crop.

They held to a course south and west below the Platte, moving farther away from the river bottoms, searching always for the most rugged, unsettled terrain to travel.

They were cautious men. Bartlett had to give them that, but they were not of the sort that he desired a long association with. He had known a lot of men in his time, good and bad, but they had all been men to ride the river with, not backshooters and women molesters like these.

He knew he had made a mistake when he had thrown his lot with these two, but he had been unable to resist the money. He was not a young man anymore, and he figured it would probably be the last large lump sum to fall his way, and he had best take it while the taking was good.

Now he was not so sure. These men were killers, the likes of which, in the old days, would have been shot by their own kind. He had already asked them once to give him his cut of the money so that Little Swallow and himself could saddle their own pony, but the request had been refused. The one called Moses had told him that he wanted to put some miles between them and Jim Winchester before they stopped to count money.

Amos Bartlett, with the passing of this summer, would be sixty-nine years old, and in part he attributed his old age to being a careful man and a good judge of character. His good judgment had not failed him, either. His better sense had warned against saddling with these men, but he had desperately wanted the five thousand dollars offered him. With it, he figured he could live out the last of his days in comfort.

All he had to do, they had told him, was to switch jugs on Strawbridge when he showed up at Winona with the money. It had been a cleverly executed trick, Bartlett admitted, and had come off without a hitch. Now he only wanted what was rightfully his, for he had earned it. He wanted his money, and he wanted to get his tail away from these killers before something went wrong.

They rode all day and all night following Pete's meeting with Winchester below the ferry. They had not counted on the bounty hunter. He had been a surprise to all of them, and they were running scared, for Winchester's reputation was known by all of them.

Just before dawn of the morning of their all night ride, Bartlett left Little Swallow behind and urged his mule up alongside the man called Pete.

"You believe he's back there, don't you?" Bartlett said.

Pete gave the old man a disgusted look in the semi-darkness. "Course he is."

"You don't suppose he heeded yore warnin'?"

"Why, hell, no. I never expected him to. Winchester don't scare that easy. I know him. All I did was let him know how I felt about him trackin' me."

Bartlett nodded. "I learned a little about him, back at the ferry. Hiram and them river rats nigh killed him, and he went right back after them. He'll be after us, too, I reckon."

"Goddamn right, he will be. I never knew Jim Winchester to run gun-shy of anybody. I knew him down in Arizona and New Mexico, and he's one hard-headed son-of-a-bitch. Moses thinks we'll lose him, but I'll bet you my cut of the money that we'll have Winchester to kill before any of us spends a dime of it."

As the chill of the night faded and the dawn broke pink in the east, Moses Gann headed up the procession, his tall, lank frame almost dwarfing the little grulla mustang he rode.

Bartlett called out to him. "We know Winchester's back there. I say we split up. Give me my cut an' Little Swallow and me will turn south. He won't know which trail to follow."

"Shut up!" Moses snapped. "We stay together for now. You'll get your money when there's time."

"There's more safety in numbers where Winchester is concerned," Pete said. "He loves a split trail. That way, he could pick us off like bird huntin', one bunch at a time."

"He didn't 'pear to be that bright to me," Bartlett grumbled. "I was a stranger to him and after he put the money in that whiskey jug he walked right out and left it there with me. All I had to do was get the other jug and switch 'em."

"Everybody makes mistakes, I guess," Pete said, "even Winchester. That don't mean he'll make another one. Don't sit too easy in your saddle."

Still grumbling, Bartlett dropped back alongside his Indian wife. Little Swallow was riding Robert Strawbridge's bay, the one that he had stolen from the corral before he stampeded the others.

Her deerskin skirt was hiked up on her thigh, and Bartlett scratched in his whiskers and looked long at the firm, shapely leg. He considered himself a lucky man already, having a girl like Little Swallow, who was young enough to be his granddaughter, share his blanket. All he needed to go with her was the money, and he would be a happy man to his dying day.

He had known of his wife's going to Winchester's bed that night at the ferry, but he had said nothing to either of them. He was not so young anymore, not always able to fill a hot-blooded filly's needs. Oh, he hadn't lost it completely—he had his better days, but they didn't come nearly so often as they used to.

Bartlett did not hold it against her. He remembered what it was like to be young and so horny you could bust. But there were other things more important to him now. Little Swallow was a fine cook, and she warmed his bed good on a cold, winter night.

There was one thing, however, that her bedding with Winchester had taught him. He knew with a certainty that he had to have that five thousand dollars if he aimed to hold onto Little Swallow. She could have any other man she wanted, and hear nothing of it from him, but he wanted her to remain under his roof.

Another thing that the long years had taught him was foresight. He had not had that foresight when he was younger, and he was feeling the effects of it now. But he realized presently that with the passing of a few more winters he was going to need that Indian girl, and by damn, he meant to hold onto her.

With the coming of daybreak, the party holed up in a stand of scrub oak and plum bush at the base of a secluded knoll. The Missouri lay fifty or more miles behind them, and the Platte half that distance to the north.

They picketed their horses on the scant grass among the plum bushes and made a cold camp, ate tinned beef with nothing to wash it down with and rolled into their blankets beneath the shade of the oaks.

Bartlett awoke in the afternoon and sat up uneasily. It was the heat that had awakened him. With the blanket around his shoulders he had sweated profusely.

The sun had just started moving into its western trajectory, and it was unbearably hot. Bartlett looked up and saw a pair of vultures circling lazily in the brassy, prairie sky.

He looked around him. Pete and Moses lay fifteen

157

feet to his left, sleeping. Between the two men lay the saddlebag that contained the money. Moses had broken the whiskey jug and stuffed the twenty thousand in his saddlebags.

Bartlett turned his gaze to Little Swallow on his right and saw that her eyes were open, watching him. He winked at her, and she gave him a half-hearted smile, a fearful smile, as if she knew what he was thinking . . . and she probably did.

It was an idea born out of desperation. Their two comrades had doublecrossed the man called Hiram, and it was just as well, for Bartlett had not liked him. Doubtlessly, the man was dead now, for Pete had given Winchester directions to the dugout where Hiram had been holding the girl.

The trouble with that action, though, was that it had created suspicion in Amos Bartlett's mind. He had lived for many years, and not without reason. He was nobody's fool, and he had no reason to believe that these men did not have the same fate in mind for him.

Bartlett threw back the blanket and tugged on his boots. He moved over beside Little Swallow. "Go saddle the two best horses," he whispered, "and be quiet about it. Leave my mule be. We're going to need some good legs and wind under us."

The Indian girl asked no questions; she moved to do as she was told. She took up two saddles, careful not to make any noise, saddled Strawbridge's bay for herself and Pete's big appaloosa for Bartlett.

The sleeping men did not stir.

Blow flies had already found the droppings of the horses, and they buzzed in swarms around the oak trees. Occasionally one of the sleeping men would slap at an insect that had lighted on his face.

Bartlett tiptoed over to the two men and watched them for a moment. The one called Pete was snoring softly, lying on his back. Moses was on his side, his face hidden from view as he had pulled the blanket over it to guard against the flies.

Pete's hands were where Bartlett could see them, but he could not see Moses' face or hands. Was the man asleep? Surely he was, for he had not moved a muscle since Bartlett had been watching him.

The old man gripped the ancient Greener tightly in his right hand. He would just have to take his chances. If he won the gamble, it would be well worth it. If he lost, well . . .

One of the horses blew suddenly and crow-hopped a little as Little Swallow attempted to tighten the cinch.

Bartlett caught his breath and looked hard at the two men on the ground, fear of being discovered rooting him to his tracks. Moses stirred slightly, then was still again.

Bartlett made a frantic gesture at Little Swallow, telling her to be still, and she did.

He waited another moment, but the men did not stir again. He took a tentative step between them . . . then another. He stretched out a hand for the saddle-bag.

Just out of reach.

He took another step, and his boot made a scuffing noise in the sand. Fear grabbed at his guts.

Pete stopped snoring.

Bartlett held his breath, and when he did he could

hear the dreadful thud of his own heart in his ears.

His hand caught the leather of the saddlebag, and he lifted it slowly, stood up with it over his arm and carefully began to back away from the sleeping men.

He looked toward Little Swallow, who was holding the horses, and grinned at her.

She started to smile in return, then suddenly, a look of horror came into her eyes. Her mouth opened to scream, but Bartlett did not hear the sound.

His eyes went back to the men on the ground, but too late. His next thought was drowned in the roar of the shot, and Amos Bartlett knew only a flash of crimson, and nothing more.

Moses simply rolled over on his back and fired from where he lay with the .44 Remington he had held under the blanket. The distance was no more than six feet, and the bullet took the old man in the right eye-socket.

Moses fired a second time, hitting Bartlett in the throat, but there was no need for it. The old man was dead long before he rolled into a heap on the ground, the saddlebag slipping from his hands.

At the sound of the first shot, Pete came to his feet, gun in hand before the second report. He stared at Bartlett, still half-asleep, then at Moses. "What th—" he began.

The sound of hoofbeats interrupted him. Little Swallow leaped astride Strawbridge's bay, laid her heels to the animal, and lit out north in the direction of the Platte. The hooves of the bay threw up clods around the base of the knoll.

Moses turned his gun toward the running horse, but Pete kicked out swiftly, hit the barrel a glancing lick of his boot toe and dislodged the weapon from the other man's hand.

Moses rubbed a stung finger. "What the hell did you do that for?"

"Let her go. She's no good to us, just a goddamn squaw, more trouble than she's worth."

"No good to you, maybe. I had use for her."

Pete shook his head. "She's no good for nothin'. She's a shittin' Indian and she'd steal you blind."

"What if she goes back to Winchester?"

"Let her. She can tell him nothing he don't already know. She was headed for the Platte, anyway—some of her people up there, probably."

Moses retrieved his gun and holstered it. He stared at the other man a long moment. Finally, he said, "Don't go bitin' off more dung than you can chew up, Pete. I'm runnin' this show an' don't you forget it. Don't ever cross me like that again, is that clear?"

Pete looked at him mildly. "Moses Gann, I've looked over a gunbarrel at many the likes of you. You can run this show till hell freezes over and it's no bother of mine, but if you want to talk tough you best be ready to back it up. I'll make you a proposition, right here and now."

Moses waited, staring at him.

"I'll let you draw out that ol' horse pistol and point it at me, and whilst you're at it I'll make you a promise. . . . I'll shoot both your eyes out before you can pull the trigger. I'll drop you right there beside that old man, and I'll take the twenty-thousand dollars and ride. What'll it be?"

Moses' face had paled a little, and he kept staring, touched a tongue to his dry lips and swallowed. "Who the hell are you?"

"Pete's good enough for you, Moses Gann. Just leave it that way." With that, the man who called himself Pete turned his back and walked toward the horses.

Moses' hand went to his gun, and he licked at his lips again. Pete kept walking, never looking back.

His hand fell away from the gun. He looked at the body of Bartlett, then at the man walking away from him. Then, suddenly, viciously, he kicked dirt at the corpse of the old man and swore.

When Robert Strawbridge got off the boat at the dock in Council Bluffs, he went directly to his tiny office on the back side of main street and collected the papers he needed. Then, avoiding any chance meeting with someone on the street, he walked the outskirts of town along the wharf to the livery stable.

He rented a horse and rode quickly out of Council Bluffs. He neither wanted to see or talk to anyone. Three days had already passed since Winchester and Rose McEachen had gone after Julia. It had taken Strawbridge until the following day to flag a steamboat and ferry out to it at Winona, and he had been lucky, at that. The steamers did not make unscheduled stops to take on passengers. He was fortunate to have been recognized by a boat's captain who knew him.

Even in stopping the boat, Strawbridge had had much explaining to do to the boat's captain that he would have preferred to have avoided. Now, he wanted to talk to no one else. There was much to do before the arrival of Julia, and he wanted the plan he had laid to remain his own. No one must even suspect.

He had been lucky when the woman, Rose McEachen, had come to him. Through her he had sent the message that he wanted to get to Winchester. Now he would not have face the man's anger himself. By the time Winchester returned to Council Bluffs, if he did, perhaps he would be cooled down.

But it did not matter. By that time the game would be played out. Julia's future would be taken care of, and Winchester's also.

Strawbridge chuckled to himself as he dismounted in front of the big house. If Amanda were alive, her mouth would fall agape at what he was planning. She had considered him a weak and spineless excuse for a man . . . well, he would show her . . . he would show them all.

There was no obstacle too large, now that his mind was set. Soon it would all be over, all his problems and all his worries. He would prove once and for all that he could handle his own problems without Amanda's support.

He went into the house and straight to his study, not even looking left or right at what he had built with the last fifteen years of his life. It did not matter anymore, the material possessions, not for him.

Even his daughter, Julia, when she learned the truth, would not believe that he had had the guts to salvage anything. But he would. He would show her. And Mr. James Winchester, when he returned, wouldn't he be surprised?

Seated at his desk, Strawbridge took up his pen

and began to write. The great, grandfather clock in the front room off his study ticked away the midafternoon hour, loud in the deathly stillness of the big house.

He wrote for almost an hour, filled out the forms he had brought from his office in town, dated and signed them, sacked them in a neat pile on his right. Then he took up a fresh, clean sheet of unlined paper, dated it at the top, and began to write again.

His usually strong, steady hand quivered a little as he worked on this document, and his breathing became heavier.

Could he do it? He swore softly to himself. What was he thinking? Of course, he could. He was as strong as any man, and they would soon all know it.

Mr. James Winchester, who thought so little of him, would have a changed opinion of Robert Strawbridge when he returned to Council Bluffs. They would all stop and take a good, long look at him when the smoke had cleared away.

If it *had* been Winchester money he had begun with, he had worked hard the last fifteen years, and he would not throw in the towel. His daughter had been no part of the original fraud, and she did not deserve to suffer for it. She *would not*! A part of what he had worked so hard for would be hers, and he meant to see to it.

He finished writing the final document, laid down his pen, and leaned back in the chair. He had only to wait now. He would wait for Julia to come, for he wanted to see her face. He owed himself that much.

And when Winchester came, it would be finished. Strawbridge reached a trembling hand for the drawer of his desk, opened it, and took out his derringer and checked the loads.

Could he do it?

Certainly.

What could be so difficult about killing a man?

Chapter 15

The sun was only an hour high when Winchester first struck the trail of his prey. He had come almost a day's ride southeast of the place where he had killed the tobacco chewer, gambling on crossing their tracks.

It was not a gamble that he had liked, but he had taken it in the interest of time. If he had ridden all the way back to Winona to take up the trail, they would have gained at least another full day on him, and he had lost enough time already in his detour for Strawbridge's daughter.

The sign that he found was not substantial. In a swale between two grassy knolls he came upon a sandy stretch of ground that the party had crossed carelessly. He dismounted to study the sign, squatted on his heels a short distance away. He did not want to leave any tracks of his own.

Four horses had crossed here, the two rear mounts obliterating some of the tracks of the first two, but he easily singled out the prints of Strawbridge's bay, Bartlett's mule, and Earl Langley's big appaloosa.

Winchester picked at his teeth contemplatively. He wondered suddenly about the game Bartlett and Little Swallow had played. He was certain they had been a part of it from the beginning. Had Bartlett known of Little Swallow's coming to his bed at the ferry? Could it have been a ruse to draw him into their confidence?

He grinned ruefully. Well, he had to admit, it had worked. Women, it seemed, were his one blind spot. But one thing was certain. If it had been a part of the plan, Little Swallow had enjoyed the playing of it.

He mounted the gray again and turned him west in the direction the party had gone. He let the horse have his head, and the gelding chose a canter for his gait.

There was no use looking for sign on the sod of the prairie. It had been too long since they had passed, and if they were smart, they would have shied away from any sandy, rocky ground and stayed on the grass.

Not that it mattered to him. A man was easy enough to follow cross-country without holding to his sign every step of the way, for a man, like any other animal, will choose the easiest route to travel.

Winchester, then, had only to do the same. Other than that he would rely chiefly on campsites and fresh horse droppings. He had discovered long ago that trying to stick to a man's tracks on the prairie was too time-consuming. While you were shambling along with your nose to the ground, the man you were tracking would ride the hell out of the country, not caring how much sign he left.

Also, not worrying with trail sign left his mind free to contemplate other things. As he rode, Winchester pondered on the events of the last three days. There was much to be considered. The news that Rose McEachen had relayed to him had shaken his uncomplicated world, and he had not yet gotten down to the business of deciding upon the best course of action when he returned to Council Bluffs.

He had never had to manage money before, at least no more than it took to pay for a hotel room or the overnight services of a cheap floozy. And he was not sure that he wanted the responsibility, either. It was nice knowing that he was wealthy, but that was about as far as it went. All that he needed or wanted was just enough to fill his pockets; the rest he would rather leave for someone else to worry about.

That lent another thought, and he snapped his fingers. That was it. Let someone else handle it, with the stipulation that he have access to money any time he wanted it. But who?

That presented another problem. The person would have to be someone he knew well and trusted, and even at that, he would be running the risk of being robbed blind.

Winchester shrugged the thought away for the time being and put his attention back on the present. He had best concentrate on Scarface and Earl Langley for now if he wanted to live to spend any of that money.

Langley. Every time he spoke the name something twisted at his guts. Was he afraid of the man? Possibly, but the fact that he might be did not disturb him. A man who knew no fear was a fool, and Winchester preferred to think of it as being merely cautious.

He could not be too cautious, either. Scarface was probably no slouch with a gun himself, and Winchester knew of Earl Langley's capabilities first hand. They had ridden together once for a spread in New Mexico, and he was a man to have on your side in any kind of a fight.

Langley was hell on wheels with a six-gun, a dead shot with either hand, and he would not be beaten in four counties with a rifle, from almost any distance you cared to name. He would not hesitate to shoot, either. He was a cold, calculating man, a hard man who, like Winchester, had lived so long with death that he did not fear it, but merely accepted it as a likelihood of his existence.

The one thing that Winchester did not fear from Langley, however, was ambush. When he had known him in New Mexico, he had been a man to ride the river with. Langley would face any man alive in a fair contest, but he would shoot no one in the back. He was that kind of a man, one of the old breed, of which there were few left.

Winchester had an ominous foreboding that in the end it would be Langley and himself, looking one another in the eye, hands poised for the draw. He didn't like that notion worth a damn and would avoid it if he could.

Was Langley still the man he had known in New Mexico? If he was, a showdown between them would probably be avoided, for he would work as hard to avoid it as Winchester himself would. But there was no guarantee that Langley was still that same man. Men could change, for the better or worse, and often had.

That evening, Winchester pulled the gelding up for a breather at a copse of cottonwood atop a rise. The party he was following had also stopped here to rest their horses. The dung droppings and other indications of their passage he estimated to be not more than a day old.

But a day was a day. A man could travel many miles in a twenty-four hour period, depending on the endurance of his horse and his own determination. With a day's ride on him, it could well be a matter of three or four days before he caught them, if then.

He left the gelding to crop some grass and walked to the top of the knoll a few yards from the cottonwoods and looked over his backtrail. It was an old habit of his, and not a bad one in any man's country. The lay of the land never looked the same going as it had coming, and anyone who had ever gotten themselves lost on the plains or in the mountains could tell you that.

It was almost second nature for Winchester to take coordinates, and he looked around him in all directions. To the north lay the muddy Platte, and to the east the Missouri. Two hundred or more miles west lay the forks where the great Platte divided into its north and south tributaries. If Scarface and Langley held to their southwesterly course, it would take them soon to the Republican, and Winchester was guessing that they would follow that stream into Colorado.

It would be a long, grueling ride to the mountains, but it was where he would go if he were carrying twenty-thousand stolen dollars and there was someone after him.

He turned his gaze east again briefly, and was about to walk back down to his horse when something caught his eye.

A movement in the distance . . . or was it?

He looked again and caught the flash of the sun off something shiny . . . saddle leather . . . a boot spur? Who could be back there? And if someone were, who would be following him? Who was left who had an interest remaining? Julia and Rose McEachen had ridden for Council Bluffs, and it could not be Strawbridge, for he had no interest other than his daughter.

Or did he?

Winchester watched for another several minutes, but he saw nothing else. Shrugging it off, he walked back down to his horse. Probably just coincidence, a lone rider out on his own business, some sodbuster, likely.

He mounted up and rode on, holding loosely to the dim trail and occasional horse droppings. With the coming of night, he chose a secluded place between low hills for his camp, so that a small fire could not be seen for any distance.

Just before he made his camp for the night, he saw movement behind him again in the growing dusk, and his suspicions grew stronger. Was the hunter also the hunted?

He built himself a hatful of fire, quickly fried some bacon and tinned beans and ate. There was no water for coffee, and he washed down the scant meal with a couple of swallows of water from his canteen.

After he had eaten, it was completely dark, and he doused his fire and carried his bedroll a few hundred yards away and rolled it out in the grass.

He disliked sleeping without the benefit of a fire, for snakes on the prairie were fearsome. But he would risk it this once. Whoever was back there might be friend or foe, but he could not afford to gamble.

He rolled up in his blanket without taking his boots off and lay awake far into the night, listening, but he never detected a sound that was out of place. The prairie wind sighed endlessly, chilling him in the hours just before dawn, but there was no other sound.

With the coming of day, breaking cold and pink in the east, Winchester arose and saddled the gelding. He caught up his blankets and went to roll his camp gear in them. It was then that he knew something was not right.

In the pan that he had eaten his meal from the night before he had left a little of the beans and a small piece of hardtack. When he picked up the pan he saw that the leftovers were gone.

A gopher perhaps? Not likely. A rodent would have left sign of his presence behind him, a few crumbs and maybe droppings in the pan. But this was not the case. What he saw was evidence of a human hand. His supper had been cleaned up; there were swipe marks where the last of the grease had been mopped up with the bread, and then a finger had been used to finish the job.

He scanned the area thoroughly, and the sign that he found was fresh, not more than a couple of hours old, but there was little of it. Only a broken stem here, some crushed blades of grass there. An untrained eye would have missed it completely.

Then, about fifty yards from his camp, he discovered a track. There wasn't much of it, just the outside edge of what looked like a moccasin print. But it was only a faint line in the dust, not enough to determine who its owner had been, or the size of him.

Winchester finished packing up, mounted the gray, and rode out briskly, disturbed a little at what he had discovered. If his visitor had meant him harm, surely he would have tried to deal his hand while at the camp. But the visitor had done nothing but eat his leftovers and vanish.

He did not understand it, and it worried him. Who could be so hungry that they had followed him for miles just to steal the scraps left from his meal?

The strangeness of it frightened him a little, and he laid his heels to the gelding, intending to put some miles between himself and his night visitor. His skin crawled to think that someone had visited his camp without arousing either him or his horse. They could have slit his throat without ever waking him. Who the hell in this country was capable of that kind of stealth? If he were down among the shadowy Apaches in Arizona, he would believe it, but not here in Nebraska.

As the morning wore on, Winchester slowed his pace a little and began to check his backtrail, but he saw nothing but empty prairie behind him.

Suddenly, as they approached a low rise bristling at the bottom with growth of oak and plum bushes, the gray began to snort with alarm and crow-hop a little.

Winchester laid a hand on the horse's neck to calm

him. "Easy, boy. What's the matter now?"

The animal snorted again but ceased to buck. Winchester dismounted and looked around. Several vultures wafted in the empty blue above, but he paid no attention to them. There were always buzzards.

What he noticed next, though, were the flies. They literally swarmed about the oaks and plum bushes, too many for the horse droppings to be their only attraction.

He left the horse tied to a bush and walked warily toward the copse of oaks. As he drew near the trees he caught a waft of the sickening, sweet smell on the air and knew what lay ahead.

The closer he came, the more unbearable the smell. He touched his tongue to his fingers and wet the ends of his nostrils, and when that no longer helped, he pinched his nose with a thumb and forefinger.

That wasn't a dead horse or any other kind of animal up there; it was a dead man. There was no other smell in the world like that, and one that Winchester had smelled before. The odor was unmistakable.

He located the body crumpled up in the edge of the trees, already swollen in an advanced state of decomposition due to the hot weather. Flies were everywhere, literally covering the body, a dark blanket of them.

Winchester remained there only long enough to kick the stiff corpse over with his foot and look at the face.

It was Amos Bartlett, or what was left of him. He had been shot in the neck, and once in the head.

Winchester felt a pang of pity. What a damned

shame—an old man like that. Despite the way Bartlett had tricked him at the ferry, Winchester could not hate him.

He left the body and went to locate where the horses had been picketed. In any other climate he would have assumed that Bartlett had been dead two or three days, but due to the hot, summer sun he would not guess that long in this instance. The old man had probably been shot not more than twenty-four hours ago.

Winchester found himself hating Scarface more than ever, if it were possible, and Earl Langley as well. Regardless of what Langley had been in New Mexico, he had been party to this from the beginning. The rape of Amanda Strawbridge, the kidnapping of Julia, and now the killing of this old man.

Langley had told him that he had nothing to do with the rape, but he had damned well stood by and watched it, and as far as Winchester was concerned, a decent man who could stand for something like that wasn't worth the lead it would take to fill his stinking hide.

He located the place where the party had hobbled their horses, and found where the trail separated. The tracks of Strawbridge's bay went north, and at a dead run it looked like. Two other sets of tracks, one of them the big appaloosa, continued west. Bartlett's mule had been cut loose, and he had merely wandered off, riderless.

If that was Little Swallow on the bay horse, she had run from them after the killing of Bartlett, and they had not pursued. Obviously, Scarface and Langley were still in possession of the money.

Winchester mounted the gray and continued west, and after a couple of miles, the trail started to angle north toward the Platte. It was a puzzling twist, but he did not worry over it. If they were headed for the river they had their reasons — maybe a hideout up there, or perhaps they were going to meet someone.

Where had Little Swallow gone after she left them? At first Winchester put the thought aside as unimportant, but then thought better of it. Could Little Swallow have been his night visitor? If so, why was she dogging him? He would have thought she would have remained with Scarface, since he was the man with the money.

He stopped the gray suddenly and turned, checking his backtrail. Once again, he thought he saw a movement back there, three miles or more away, and he swore softly. If he didn't know better, he would feel like he was being boxed, riding into a trap.

His subconscious sounded a warning bell in his mind, but he put the feeling off on his overly-suspicious nature and rode on.

Robert Strawbridge was standing in front of the big window upstairs when he spotted the buggy coming up the river road. He was dressed in his best suit and tie, shoes shined to perfection, and the thin crown of hair on the back of his head neatly combed.

His heart was pounding heavily, but he had lost none of his determination. How could he ever face Julia now that the secret of his success was out? She had always believed him to be an honest man, a self-made man, her father, the successful entrepreneur, the riverboat tycoon.

The big window on the second floor provided an excellent view of the river that moved sluggishly southward, reflections of the late summer sun dancing off its surface. In the distance, he could see the outlying buildings of Council Bluffs, and he stood there for a long minute, just looking toward the river town that he had loved and prospered in.

A sob racked his body suddenly, and perspiration appeared on his forehead. He wiped at his eyes with clammy hands and tried to control himself.

The buggy on the road was drawing near, and Strawbridge squinted to get a look at the two riders on the seat. He could barely make out their faces from here, but he supposed that he had seen enough.

He turned away from the window quickly and went downstairs. He fumbled for the only object he had in his pockets now, a key, and went to the gun cabinet.

The derringer idea he had already discarded . . . too ineffective. He opened the gun cabinet and took out his new model Winchester .30-.30. He smiled suddenly at the irony; the name of this rifle and James Winchester were the same. To his knowledge, though, the gun's manufacturer and his nephew were not related.

Strawbridge made sure the rifle was loaded and went out of the house by the back door. He could hear the sounds of the horse and buggy on the road now. He could wait no longer.

Behind the house were two deep ravines that ran a course into a wooded area just off the river. He took the first ravine he came to and was soon out of sight of the house, headed into a thick grove of water oak and cottonwood.

He walked what he considered to be about a mile from the house and stopped to listen. No sound came to him but that of the river and the wind in the cottonwoods.

There were no shouts . . . no one calling for him.

Did he expect it?

His forehead broke out in sweat again, and he wiped at it angrily. It was too late now . . . too late for any of them.

They would soon know what Robert Strawbridge was made of. Very soon they would all know, and they would be sorry.

It was the last thing he could do to prove himself. His daughter would love him for his bravery, and Winchester would at last come to respect him.

If Amanda were here he knew she would advise against this. If she were still alive Winchester would not yet know the truth, for Amanda would say, "What do you mean, tell the truth? Give up all that you've worked for? Are you crazy? He'll never find out, I tell you—never!"

Well, he had found out. He, Robert Strawbridge, had told him . . . and now there was nothing left to do but finish it, do what he had come here to do.

Was he crazy? Maybe. But his plan was laid, and he could not turn back.

Stumbling a little, tears streaming from his eyes, he walked to a deadfall and sat down on it. He could not see to unlace his shoe for the tears, so he merely forced it off.

He planted the stock of the rifle against the ground and jammed the barrel in the roof of his mouth.

His foot sought the trigger.

His heart thudded with distant thunder, and from somewhere nearby came the cry of a magpie.

His toe found the trigger, and the magpie cried again.

It was the last sound of God's earth that Robert Strawbridge heard, but for the roar that filled his ears suddenly . . . and the wind.

Chapter 16

The camp thief visited Winchester again on the following night. He discovered the evidence in the cold ashes of his supper fire, another partial moccasin print. But this time there was more.

He mounted the gray and circled his camp, looking for sign. On the first pass he found nothing, but he continued to circle, each time reaching farther out, and on the third time around he found what he was looking for.

A horse had been tethered about a quarter-mile from his fire, and the camp robber had walked from that point.

He dismounted and began to inspect the area closely, and within a few minutes, he had proven his theory correct. There, where the horse had dug in when the thief had departed, were the tracks of Robert Strawbridge's bay horse.

Little Swallow.

He was almost sure of it now, and he was also

relieved. He was not being set up, then, boxed in, as he had earlier thought. The Indian girl was just hungry, but afraid to approach him because of her part in the trickery at Winona.

Dismissing her, Winchester mounted his horse again and struck out on the trail of Scarface, still moving northwest. The morning sun was already hot on his shoulder. Only a few sparse, buttermilk clouds hung in the north, the bell-clear sky overhead promising another hot, miserable day.

The terrain had begun to flatten out around him, evidence that he was drawing near the Platte, and he had not ceased to ponder Scarface's reason for going to the river.

There must be something there for them, but Winchester had already ruled out the probability of a boat there. It would not be practical for them. He could travel faster by horseback upriver than they could in a canoe, and surely they did not intend to head back downriver, to the Missouri.

That only left him one conclusion. They either had a hideout on the river, or they were planning to meet someone there.

Who? Was there another player now that he was not aware of? Somehow Winchester did not believe it. Langley and Scarface had already double-crossed two members of their party in order to share the twenty-thousand between them. He did not think they would be willing to cut anyone else in on the take.

He held the gray gelding to a steady, ground-eating pace, but not one that would tire him quickly. The miles rolled underneath them, and by midmorning he knew that they would soon reach the Platte if they held to their present course.

He stopped just before noon to check the terrain behind him. He thought he saw something, trailing far behind, but could have been mistaken. Distance in this country was often deceiving.

A short time later, around noon, he saw the smoke . . . a rising column of it, unbroken as yet by the wind, climbing skyward.

He stopped long enough for the gray to blow and mopped the sweat from his forehead. The scorching, prairie sun hung like a torch overhead.

The smoke column was not a mile distant. Winchester could not believe that it was Scarface and Langley up there. They were not fools, and neither was he.

He was reminded of his days with the Apache in Arizona and Mexico, and the tricks that the Indians had taught him. He did not think that Earl Langley was confident enough to send up a column of smoke, for Langley knew that he was on their trail. He had to know.

It must be a trick, for they would not have been that careless. If Langley had sent up that smoke, he was trying to lead him into a trap.

He considered a moment. He would first need to find a good vantage point from which he could see their camp, and then he would exercise the Apache teachings of patience. He would watch and wait, and with luck, when they were tired of waiting for him, he could lay a trap of his own.

Urging the gray ahead, he walked the horse the last mile cautiously and dismounted near a grove of cottonwood not far from where the smoke rose.

He left the horse standing in the trees without tying him. He wanted the horse to be free to come to him should he not be able to return himself.

Winchester belly-crawled to the summit of the low knoll overlooking the camp and took in the sights below. As he had suspected, there was a cabin there, nestled in a grassy swale between low-lying hills, the river only a few miles distant.

The cabin was only a soddy, of the type common on the prairie. The column of smoke was rising from a clay chimney, but he saw no other activity.

He was facing the back of the soddy, and there was no door there, so he assumed that the only entrance was through the front. Thirty or forty yards in back of the soddy was a small corral with one horse in it, a grulla mustang that he had not seen before.

Scarface's horse? Likely. But where was the big appaloosa, and more importantly, where was Earl Langley?

Involuntarily, the skin on the back of Winchester's neck prickled, and he looked behind him. Beyond the cottonwoods where his gelding stood there was nothing. The country stretched away flat for some distance. There was no hill or plant large enough to hide a man.

Suddenly, he had an alarming thought. Might Langley have double-crossed Scarface, killed him and taken the money for himself? He swore softly. The thought angered him more than anything else. He wanted no one to deprive him of the opportunity to gun down the Scarface.

Winchester waited, sweat running streams down his face. The sun began to wester, and still he waited.

Something had to happen down there before he could move, something had to break. It was too still . . . too quiet.

He swore again, bitterly. If Scarface was lying in that soddy dead and Earl Langley gone, he was wasting eternally precious time. But what could he do? The teachings of his Apache brothers came back to him. *The warrior who hurries will always meet his end first.*

He took a deep breath and steadied himself. He would not be the one to hurry. If the men were in that soddy and did not make an appearance, he would wait for nightfall and make his move under cover of darkness.

Better, he would wait until just before the fall of night, at dusk, when the light would be just enough to see but poor for shooting. That, he reflected, would be a time for the knife.

He reached a hand to his boot to assure himself of the blade's presence. He pulled out the knife and tested its edge, then checked the loads in his Colt. The light would not be good enough for the rifle.

On the rise opposite him, sunlight reflected off something, and Winchester squinted. Was someone up there, facing the front of the soddy with a rifle?

He turned again to look behind him.

Nothing . . . only the gelding cropping prairie grass near the cottonwoods.

He watched the summit opposite him for more than an hour, but the reflection he had seen was not repeated. Had he seen anything, or had it been only a trick of the sun?

He did not think so. Someone was up there,

185

possibly Langley, watching the front of the soddy.

The day drew near its close, and still Winchester waited. Everything below him was as still as death. The sun sank in the west with fiery brilliance, sending out rosy fingers to grasp at what was left of the day.

Darkness from the east began to push against the glow, running it into hiding, and the twilight time that he had waited for gathered around him.

Still he waited, judging the light, selecting the right time. When it was right, he slipped back down the hill and skirted the base of it, approached the pole corral at an angle.

He knelt behind the scant cover of the poles a moment, studied the soddy and the knoll that lay beyond. Still there was no sign of movement.

His rifle he had left with his horse, and now he drew the Colt from the holster and ran, crouching, to the back wall of the soddy. He pressed an ear to the earthwork and listened, but he doubted that he could have heard anything through the thick layer of sod.

He went around the cabin fast and flattened himself beside the front door. He didn't like exposing himself to the knoll worth a damn, and his skin crawled. He only hoped that the gathering darkness would be good to him.

The door of the soddy was open. Light flickered inside from the flames of a dying fire, and Winchester hesitated only an instant. There was no other way open to him. He went through the door, gun in hand, expecting anything, gunfire or . . .

There was nothing. The soddy was empty but for the eerie reflections cast on the earth walls by the fire. Against the wall beside the fireplace was an unmade bunk, and on the bunk lay a pair of saddlebags.

Something in Winchester's danger-conditioned subconscious began to sound a warning bell.

Trap!

He moved out of the open doorway and peered outside into the failing light.

There was nothing out there . . . nothing at all. No movement and no sound. It was quiet . . . eerie quiet.

What the hell was in that saddlebag? He went back to the bunk, caught up the near one, and jerked open the flap.

Money . . . stuffed with it! He opened the other bag and found more of the same. He threw the bags over his shoulder and went out the door of the cabin, turned to his left and started to run.

It was then, when he least expected it, that the trap was sprung. He had not taken three steps when he heard the scuffing of feet behind him. He froze, the warning bell tolling in his mind . . . too late.

Loud came the click of a hammer being drawn back, and Winchester went for his gun, turned in desperation.

A shot cracked, and his nerves bunched, expecting the impact of a bullet, but it did not come. When he completed his turn he saw a tall, lank man partially bent over with one hand gripping his side. Blood oozed between his fingers.

The man did not fall. As Winchester stared, not comprehending what had happened, the tall man straightened up and raised his pistol for another shot, at the same time revealing the livid scar that distorted his face.

Scarface!

Winchester fired from the hip, and the bullet took the tall man in the center of his chest. He staggered with the impact of it.

The gun pointing at Winchester wavered a little, still did not fire, and Winchester shot again, then again and again at not much more than point blank range.

Scarface was literally lifted off his feet and slammed to the ground, dead before he landed. Both of the last two shots had taken him in the upper body, near the heart.

Even before the echo of the shots had died away, Winchester realized at last what had happened. He dove for the protection of the cabin wall and crouched there.

That first shot had been fired from the top of the knoll. As he had earlier thought, there *had* been a rifleman up there. But he had shot the wrong man . . . or had he?

Winchester was completely confused. He could make nothing of it. Had that been Earl Langley on the knoll? If it had, why had he shot Scarface?

Scarface had been hiding somewhere nearby, at some place he had failed to detect from the hill in back of the soddy, and the man had come up behind him when he ran out of the cabin. He would have been dead meat but for the shot from the knoll, for Scarface had had the hammer back before he even started to turn.

Why the hell would Langley shoot his own comrade? Was that even Langley up there? Could it be the party they had ridden here to meet?

Winchester started backing away from the soddy.

He reached the pole corral, and the grulla mustang snorted at him in the darkness. He went around the corral, breathed a sigh of relief as he skirted the base of the hill, and ran for his horse.

He reached the stand of cottonwoods, but his relief fell short. He looked around desperately, and once again, the hair at the back of his neck prickled a warning.

The gray was gone . . . vanished into the night, along with his rifle.

He gave a low whistle, then another one, but the horse did not come. Then, from the other side of the hill, he heard hoofbeats . . . but they were not approaching him . . . they were moving away.

He remembered the horse at the corral, the grulla mustang, and retraced his steps back there. After a lengthy search did not produce a saddle, he fashioned a hackamore from a piece of rope he found.

Slipping into the corral, he spoke soothingly to the mustang. The horse let him approach after a moment, and Winchester began to rub his head and back with his hands, letting the animal familiarize itself with his scent.

When the horse had grown accustomed to him, he slipped on the hackamore and mounted bareback. The mustang stepped a little uneasily at first, unused to being ridden without the benefit of a saddle, but he grew accustomed to it quickly enough.

It was fully dark now, the moon just beginning to rise, and Winchester walked the mustang around to the front of the soddy where he had killed Scarface.

He dismounted and looked at the man for a moment. How long had he searched? Sometimes he could not even remember anymore. And now, once again, it had amounted to nothing.

The man was lying face down on the ground, and after a moment, Winchester hooked a toe under the corpse's shoulder and rolled him over.

He stared long and bitterly at the contorted face revealed by the starlight. The anger began to mount in him, and suddenly, he kicked the lifeless body, then a second time . . . and a third.

For a period of several minutes, rage pushed every rational thought out of his mind, and Winchester kicked the dead man over and over again, kicked him until his leg was tired and he was breathing heavily from the exertion.

Finally, he stopped, but continued to look at the dead man's face bitterly. It was not the man, not the face he remembered from his boyhood, not the scarfaced horror from his dreams. This man was tall and wiry, while the man he hunted was shorter and heavy of build.

And the dead man at his feet . . . the goddamned scar was on the *wrong* side of his face!

When Winchester's nerves finally settled, he mounted the mustang again and turned him away from the soddy. He felt badly already over visiting his anger on the body of a dead man, but he had been unable to control it. He had hoped so hard and believed so completely that this time it would be him, and when it had not been . . .

Making a supreme effort, Winchester put his mind back on the present. He was in possession of the money now, but somehow he did not believe it was over. Who had been the rifleman on the knoll, and why had he shot the scarfaced man?

But the thing that worried him most was the disappearance of Earl Langley. It did not make any sense. The fact that Langley had left without his share of the money only spelled one thing . . . that he was coming back.

And when Langley returned, he would be looking for James Winchester, for he was that kind of man.

Chapter 17

He approached the back of the knoll where the rifleman had lain in wait with caution. Near the summit, he dismounted from the mustang and began to look for sign by the light of a three-quarter moon.

After a brief search, he located the spot where the marksman had bellied down in the grass, even found an indentation where his elbow had rested when he sighted his rifle, and nearby lay an empty shell casing.

Winchester backtracked down the hill, scanned the ground carefully but took his time at it. The pale glow cast by the moon was not good, and he did not want to miss anything.

He cast about at the bottom of the hill but came up empty. He climbed up on the grulla mustang and turned the horse northeast toward the river. It was then, as he was leaving the hill behind, that he saw something and stopped to inspect it closer.

What he found was a surprise, but also something of a relief. It was the tracks of Robert Strawbridge's bay.

Little Swallow, then, had been the rifleman, the one who had shot the scarfaced man from the knoll. How, he wondered, had she gotten in that position on the hill without his seeing her? He had believed that she was behind him to the east.

Well, he didn't suppose that was much to worry about. Had she not robbed his camp twice without his catching her? That Indian girl was not to be taken lightly. She was as good at what she did as any buck he had ever encountered.

But why had she wanted to help him, and where had she got the rifle? The empty casing he had picked up at the top of the hill was .30-.30 caliber. She must have stolen the gun from someone else's camp.

Winchester kept the mustang on the fresh tracks of Strawbridge's bay, riding slowly. It was an effort to hold to the trail in the semi-darkness, and when the moon went down, it would be impossible.

But he wanted to catch that girl and ask her some questions. Had she merely wanted to avenge the death of Amos Bartlett? He didn't believe it, for she had not appeared to be that fond of the man. Why she had stuck with the old buzzard he did not know, which led him to think there may have been something there that he was unaware of. You never could tell. Indians were funny that way; their reasoning often made no particular sense to anyone but them.

As he had expected, when the moonlight failed he lost the bay's trail, but kept to a northeasterly course that would take him eventually to the Platte. Little Swallow had been pointed for the river, and he figured he would cross her tracks again when morning came.

Over the next couple of hours, Winchester developed

a liking for the little grulla mustang. The gray gelding he was not, but he was a hardy little animal with good wind and plenty of staying power. What he lacked in length of leg he made up for with heart.

If he did not get the gray back he would keep the mustang. The scarfaced man would certainly have no further use for him.

Winchester pushed the horse until dawn began to tinge the eastern horizon with pink, and only then did he stop to take a breather. He watched the morning break clear and bright, the sun peeping out eagerly. It promised to be another hot one.

With the coming of light, he located the tracks of the bay horse again and within a half-hour had followed them to the river. The tracks were fresh, made only minutes ago, and he dismounted from the mustang to proceed on foot.

He could hear the movement of the river as he drew closer to it, the barely audible hum indicative of a moving body of water, and he came in sight of it only moments later.

The Platte at this point was wide and muddy, with a lot of white water on the rocks near shore. Being only a few miles from where it divided to become the North and South Platte, the river was shallow enough here that a man could almost wade across it.

Somewhere not far off, he thought he heard a voice amid the noises of the river, someone singing. He kept walking but kept his distance from the river's edge, not wanting her to see him first. If he should surprise her she just might take a shot at him, and she had already proven herself no slouch with a rifle. She had nailed the scarfaced man back there from the top of the hill, and it had been a downhill shot in bad light.

Another hundred yards, and he saw Strawbridge's bay ground-haltered among some stunted willows not far from the riverbank. He went to the horse and spoke low to calm the animal. The bay remembered him and barely flicked an ear.

The singing was close by now, a woman's voice raised in some Indian tongue that he had not heard before, probably Mandan. The voice came from the water's edge, along with some splashing that was not being done by the river.

The early morning air still bore a chilled quality held over from the night, and Winchester shivered a little at the sound of the splashing. "Hell of a time for a bath," he murmured.

The bay horse flicked another ear, agreeing with him.

He went toward the cloak of foliage that shielded the side of the river and found a good vantage point among the willows. Directly below was a shallow pool of still water off the river where a section of the bank had washed out in some past flood.

The scene in the pool was a fascinating one, and Winchester sat down on his heels and watched for some time. The girl had her back to him as she splashed water over herself, singing loud and nasally, a sound obviously intended for no one's ears but her own.

The water where she stood was not quite waist deep, and it did not hide the graceful swell of her buttocks before they dipped out of sight beneath the surface. Her long, straight hair was raven black, and her skin a golden brown.

Almost immediately, Winchester decided that he had

not had enough time at Winona to sufficiently appreciate this creature. That was a little detail that he would need to attend to over the next few days. It was a long way back to Council Bluffs and Rosie McEachen. He grinned. He was sure Rose would understand, anyway.

Little Swallow finished her splashing finally and turned to walk out of the pool. He stood up with a guilty grin plastered across his face, and she saw him.

She gave a little start, and her mouth dropped open, but other than that she showed little agitation. She just stood there in the knee-deep water and looked at him, chin lifted, unashamed.

Her small breasts rode high and firm, the nipples hard and pointed from the cold water. The only thing that marred her bronze beauty was the patch of bushy black in the middle that dripped water between her legs.

Winchester just stood and stared, too, appraising her shamelessly. At last, though, he stepped down to the bank and extended a hand. "Better get outa there before you catch your death."

She took his hand nobly, like any fully-dressed, elegant lady, shivering a little as the cold morning pimpled her flesh. Her deerskins were hanging on a bush, and she put them on while he watched.

"I will not—catch death—as you say, Mister Winchester," Little Swallow said, in her halting English. "I have bathed in the river every day of my life, an' never sick, cold days or hot."

"You, maybe. Me, I'd die of pneumonia before the week was out."

She shook her head vigorously. "You try, you see . . . not die."

He grinned. "Well, maybe I will sometime, at that! You an' me together, huh?"

She smiled but would not meet his eyes, directed her gaze shyly at the ground. "That would be good, Win—chester."

He walked to her, took her chin in his hand and lifted it. She met his eyes hesitantly. "I owe you one, girl. You saved my bacon back there, you know that?"

Little Swallow looked puzzled. "Saved—bacon?"

"You know, saved my hide when you shot the scar-faced man."

She acted as if she understood. "Scarface man," she said, "bad hombre—killed Amos—shot brains out."

"That's right, Little Swallow. He was a bad hombre, but he's a dead hombre now, thanks to you."

Again she was puzzled. "What I do?"

"When you shot him back there, with the rifle," he said impatiently.

"I shoot nobody," she answered. "No rifle."

Winchester took her by the arm and led her away from the river back to Strawbridge's bay. He looked at the horse and saw that what she had said was true. He had not noticed when he first came, but there was no rifle on the bay horse, not even a sheath for one.

He grabbed the Indian girl by the shoulders and jerked her close to him. "If it wasn't you who shot the scarfaced man, what were you doing there? I found your horse's tracks. I know you were there!"

He saw fear mingled with pain in her eyes, and suddenly realized that he was squeezing her arms. He relaxed his grip a little.

"I hear shots," she said. "I went—to see. I hear horses riding away—I saw you running away—from the cabin. I saw a dead man—that is all. It is all I saw."

Winchester released her and let his arms fall limp at his sides. If Little Swallow had not been the rifleman on the knoll, who had?

Langley?

But why? And where in hell had he gone?

What—?

Then, as he stood there looking at the Indian girl, he saw her eyes grow large with fear . . . and she was looking past his shoulder.

The hair at the back of his neck gave its prickly final warning, and he turned slowly, deliberately, and saw the man standing not twenty feet behind him.

It was Earl Langley.

"You must be slippin', Jim. I don't ever remember a time when I could walk up on you like that."

The man's voice was conversational, almost friendly, but Winchester detected the dangerous undertone that he had heard only once before, long ago.

Langley's arms dangled loosely at his sides, the right hand only inches from the butt of his gun, but Winchester was looking at something else—something he had not seen before.

Earl Langley's eyes were not the eyes he remembered. They looked tired and were half-closed, and there was a deathly, cold quality about them that shivered Winchester to his boot soles. They were eyes such as he had never wanted to look into, and if he lived to tell the tale, never wanted to look into them again.

Langley's face was drawn and haggard, his mouth pinched and tight. He was not the same man whom Winchester had known in New Mexico.

"I guess maybe I am, Earl," he said. "A man can go

soft, hangin' out with the settlement folk."

"Get you killed, too," Langley said. "You'd be a dead man right now, if I'd've been a dry-gulcher. But I've never shot a man in the back in my life, Jim. You believe it?"

Winchester nodded. "I know you're not a back-shooter, Earl. You don't have to prove anything to me."

"Always knew it would come to this, though. I knew it way back, down in New Mexico, I knew it. We're among the last of our kind, Winchester. And if I was to know I was to get myself shot, I'd like for it to be a man like you what did the shootin', not some dry-gulcher like Moses Gann and that bunch."

"He wasn't my man, Earl," Winchester said. "Moses wasn't the Scarface."

"I'm sorry as hell, Jim."

"I'll find him one day, don't worry."

Langley shook his head. "I wisht you did have the time for it, Jesus, I do!"

"I've got the time, Earl."

Langley met his eyes across the distance that separated them. "It's not that easy, boy. You've got something that belongs to me, and I mean to have it. I don't want to do it, Jimmy, but I can take you . . . believe me, I can."

The tension was getting to Winchester. He breathed heavily, and the palms of his hands were sweating. Was he scared of Earl Langley? In the same instant that he asked the question he knew the answer.

This was a thoroughly dangerous man he faced, not just some tinhorn who fancied himself a gunman. Those kind were a dime a dozen, but men of the sort Earl Langley had once been came few and far between.

Had once been? Well, perhaps the quality of his character had diminished, but his skill with weapons would not have.

"It doesn't have to be this way, Earl," he said. "You can ride out . . . just ride out and forget it."

"Can't do it, boy. I'm not a young man anymore. I've got to have a stake for myself. I've got a wife an' kid down in New Mexico, did you know that?"

Winchester blinked. He had not known it.

"Yeah, I got me a wife an' kid. She's Mexican, but hell, she's good to me, and that's all that matters, ain't it? I mean to go back down there and settle down, but I've got to have a stake for her an' my kid. Somethin' to start on, you know?"

"I know, but this ain't the right —" Winchester stopped in mid-sentence. He saw Langley's eyes change . . . the signal.

"No, Earl," he shouted, *"don't do it!"*

Langley went for his gun and he was fast . . . incredibly fast. The gun belched fire, and Winchester felt the bullet whip air near his cheek before he even cleared leather.

But then his own gun was out and blazing. He saw Langley stagger, but he did not go down. Langley fired again, and something burned Winchester's neck.

Winchester fanned the hammer of his Colt, emptied his gun into Langley's chest, and the holes that appeared magically in the man's overall bib spurted blood.

Langley went to his knees, but he was not dead. He lifted his gun and fired again, so fast that Winchester did not have time to blink.

A hot iron ran its searing path through his left side,

and Winchester doubled over with it and pitched sideways as his own finger tightened on the trigger, but the hammer fell on a spent cartridge. His gun was empty.

He raised his head from the ground and looked at Langley. The man was still on his knees, looking at him over his pistol barrel.

Winchester heard himself praying, uttering words that came strangely to the lips of a man such as he, but as he looked at Langley, the glaze of death veiled the man's eyes, and he pitched forward on his face. His outstretched hand still gripped his gun.

Winchester rolled over on his back and stared up at the brassy sky. He wondered if it was coincidence, or if someone up there had heard him.

Little Swallow came to him, and he looked at her. "He shot me," he told her numbly. "I put six bullets in his chest, and he still shot me."

She did not answer, and her silence alarmed him. He looked suddenly, fearfully, at Langley's body, half expecting to see him getting up.

Chapter 18

Little Swallow cleansed and bandaged his wounds, and Winchester was on his feet by the next day, in pain, but able to move around.

The bullet wound in his side was superficial, barely catching the flesh and passing clean through. The bullet burn on his neck was nothing more than a scratch. He had been lucky.

Every time he recalled the confrontation with Langley, a cold chill passed over him. It was the closest brush with death that he had ever had. Langley had beaten his draw cleanly, and would have killed him if only he had placed his shots better.

Had Langley missed his shots purposely? Had he committed suicide?

Winchester was not sure. It was hard to believe a man like Earl Langley could have missed after beating him to the draw, but nothing was impossible in a gunfight.

The man had been under a strain. He had gleaned

that from their conversation before the fight, and some of the things he had said sounded like a man very troubled.

Why had Langley stopped Scarface from killing him back at the cabin? Langley had said that death at the hands of a man like Scarface was not an honorable death for men like Winchester and himself.

Was that the thinking of a sound mind? Winchester did not think so, but he also had trouble believing that Langley had thrown the gunfight, that he had wanted to die, that he had wanted Winchester to kill him. Somehow he could not accept it.

But there was no need of worrying about it. Only Earl Langley knew the answer, and he would never tell. It was just water under the bridge now. He had twenty-thousand dollars in the bags behind his saddle, and Earl Langley was only another dead man.

On the morning of the second day on the Platte, when he could walk upright with his side wound, Winchester found where Langley had left his horses, not far from the river.

He found Langley's mount, along with his own gray gelding, and the remainder of the puzzle fell into place. After Langley had shot Scarface from the knoll, he had ridden around and caught up the gelding, intending to put Winchester on foot. He had evidently forgotten Moses Gann's mustang in the pole corral behind the cabin.

Winchester turned Langley's horse loose, but kept the grulla mustang. He had developed a liking for that horse.

Since he was unable to dig a grave, he dragged Langley's body into a draw just off the river and tumbled a bank off on him. It was the best he could do, and Langley was lucky to get that.

Afterward, he went back to Little Swallow, and they rode out down the river. She had relatives on the Platte, or so she said, and asked if she might ride with him until they reached her kin.

In view of the fact that she was not a stranger, and the only woman within fifty miles, Winchester consented, with the condition that she administer to his wounds along the way, which she did, along with sundry other necessities.

The trip upriver was not entirely a chore, and at their parting on the Platte, he made a gift to her of Robert Strawbridge's bay horse. He figured it was the least he could do considering all she had done for him.

She was genuinely grateful, and surprised. Tears filled her dark eyes, for she had seldom been shown any gratitude for anything she had done in her life.

He suggested to her that he might be back that way soon, and from the look she gave him, he knew she believed it. He felt badly, riding away, but Rose McEachen was waiting in Council Bluffs, and unfinished business.

Winchester's hand strayed often to the saddlebags behind him. He liked the feeling it provided. There would always be money when he wanted it now, more where this came from, or so he believed. It had been a strange idea to get used to, at first, but it was growing on him.

On a bright, clear Sunday morning he took the river road that would lead him to the Strawbridge house. He rode the gray gelding and led the grulla mustang, and when they took the road, the gray began to step quickly, sensing a feed and rest ahead.

When they came in sight of the house, Winchester drew the gray up a moment, not knowing what to make of what he saw. There was a crowd of people up there in front of the house, and a large number of horses and buggies lining the road.

He patted the gray's neck. "What we got here, boy, a church social?"

They rode near the house, and at last he singled out Rose McEachen from the crowd. She noticed him finally, sitting his horse by the road, and walked out to him.

He dismounted from the gray, and she embraced him briefly.

"I see you made it."

"Yeah, I got lucky, one more time."

"I'm glad. Did you get your man?"

"Not the right man. I killed a man with a scar on his face, but he wasn't the man I've been looking for. He wasn't Scarface."

Her face fell. "It's not over, then, is it." It was more a statement than a question.

"No," he said, "It's not over. There was always the possibility that it wasn't him—you know that."

"What about Earl Langley?"

"He's dead."

"But you'll be moving on, won't you?"

"Got to, Rosie. But I'll find him one day, you'll see. And then it *will* be over."

"Will it, Jim?" she said bitterly. "Will it really?"

He changed the subject, pointed to the people in front of the house. "What's going on here?"

"Robert Strawbridge killed himself. They found his body in back of the house yonder. Blew the top of his head off with a rifle."

"Jesus! What the hell for?"

"We're not sure. He left Julia a letter explaining, but she hasn't told much of what he said, yet — only something about all the pressure he was under, that he didn't want to face her after she found out what he and her mother had done."

"Is that all?" He was dumbfounded.

"No. She also said that he was afraid you would take him to court when you returned, that you would ruin him."

It was his turn to be disappointed. "Ah, I see. It's all off now, isn't it? Since he shot himself the truth will never be told, and I'll get nothing, right?"

"No, it's not that way at all. You see, he also left a will. He prepared everything on his desk before he killed himself. He left everything to you, all the major assets, and all the stock. But there's one stipulation."

"What's that?"

"He arranged a profit-sharing plan. The business is totally yours, but Julia is to receive a share of the profits from it."

"And if I don't agree?"

"I've already talked to a lawyer in Council Bluffs about that."

He grinned. "You always did have a head for business, Rosie."

She nodded. "I figured you'd ask that, and the lawyer said that if you contested the will the whole thing might eventually go up for grabs. The decision would probably be tied up in litigation for years in the courts. Your best bet would be to take it the way Strawbridge left it."

"Then I guess he won in the end, didn't he?"

"If you want to call it that. I hardly would."

"Looks like we've got our work cut out for us here, doesn't it?"

"We?"

"Sure, we." He put an arm around her shoulder. "I've been thinkin' about things the last few days, Rosie, and I've come to a decision. I've got a business to run here, but I'm going to have to be away a lot, see, and like I said, you always did have a good head for business."

"But —"

"No buts. I remember you tellin' me long ago that you'd like to have a chance to run your own business, a social club, you were talking about then. And this is even better, more respectable."

"But what about you?"

"Oh, I'd check in on you from time to time."

Rose McEachen's face was glowing. "Would you, Jim?"

"It's a promise." He took her arm, and they walked up to the big house together.